The Invisible Soul Anthology

Healing With Words

George Beasley

GB
GEORGE BEASLEY
AUTHOR

ISBN (digital): 979-8-9967437-6-6
ISBN (paperback): 979-8-9967437-0-4
ISBN (hardcover): 979-8-9967437-1-1

Library of Congress Control Number: 2026919516

Editing by Sandra Wester

Illustrations by Lisa Beasley

Publishing by Elizabeth's Writing Corner
https://www.elizabethswritingcorner.com/

E

The greatest blessing of writing this anthology has been the beautiful soul sitting right by my side as each story unfolded. Together, we uncovered the clues to my healing, and we continue to walk this path of discovery hand in hand. Today, July 28, 2026, marks our forty-second anniversary. The letter my Sweet Lisa gave me this morning speaks volumes of the profound love that guides our journey. With all my heart, this anthology is dedicated to my beautiful Sweet Lisa. **AGTG.**

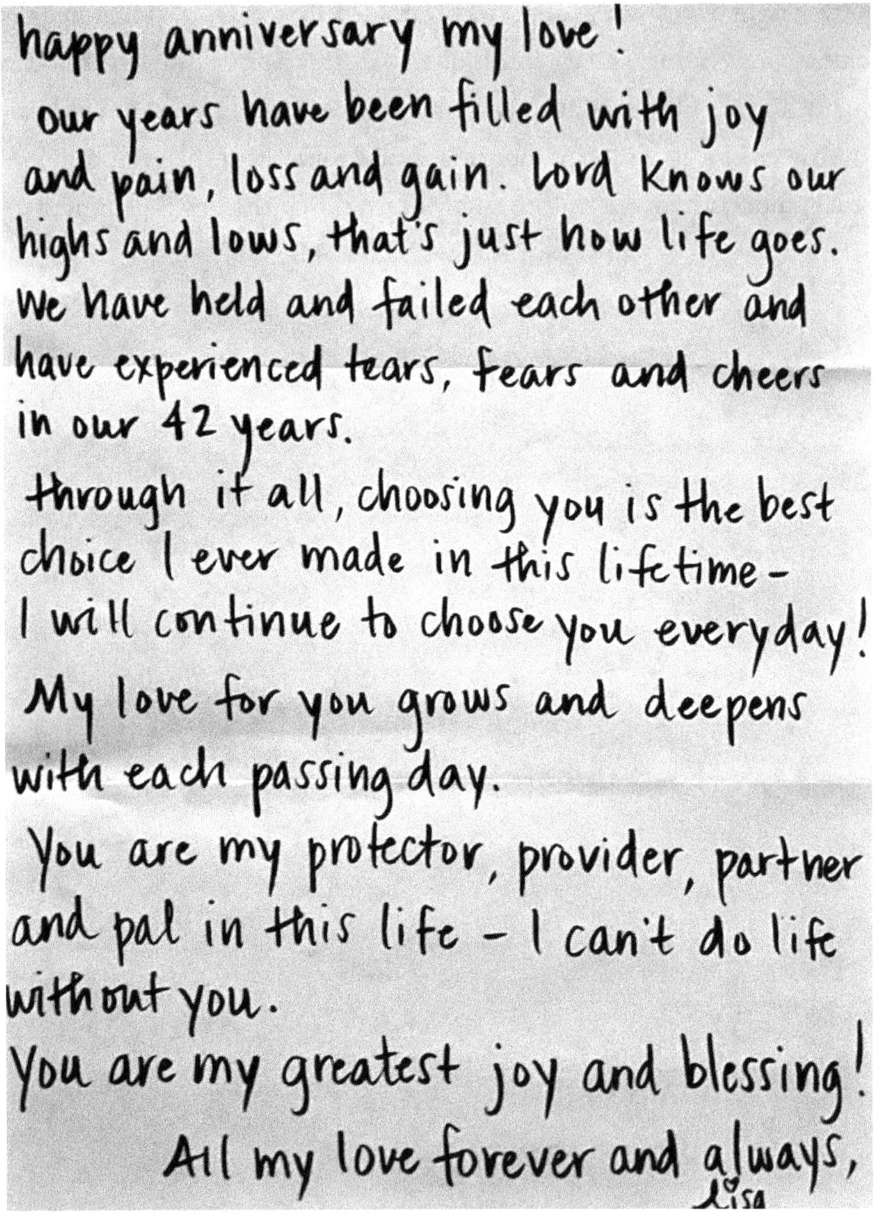
happy anniversary my love!

our years have been filled with joy and pain, loss and gain. Lord knows our highs and lows, that's just how life goes. We have held and failed each other and have experienced tears, fears and cheers in our 42 years.

through it all, choosing you is the best choice I ever made in this lifetime - I will continue to choose you everyday!

My love for you grows and deepens with each passing day.

You are my protector, provider, partner and pal in this life - I can't do life without you.

You are my greatest joy and blessing!

All my love forever and always,

Lisa

Silence is deaf in the mist of great storms.
All you can hear is the rumble of thunder.
The voices scream death.
Your will to live is disappearing.

Where am I?
Who can hear me?
It's dark in the silence.

Invisible, when so many are looking.
All I can see is darkness.
They see, but they won't help me.

Where am I?
Who can see me?
It's dark being unseen.

There is one who can hear;
There is one who can see.

Where is He?
He is here.
What is His Name?

Jesus, The Son of God.

Contents

Preface

This atmospheric and introspective prologue introduces *The Invisible Soul Anthology*, setting the stage for stories about the quiet moments, hidden struggles, and profound everyday miracles that often go unnoticed in modern life.

Words bring healing, and healing brings new life. New life brings new words.

Life never stops to watch its own reflection. It hurries past coffee shops in the morning and glances blindly at rain-slicked neon by night. In this rushing sea of humanity, some people walk like ghosts—holding heavy burdens, secret passions, and quiet triumphs that never make the headlines.

This anthology is a collection of those untold stories. It is an invitation to pause, look closely, and listen to the whispers of the human experience that are usually drowned out by the noise of the world. Stop scrolling for a minute, and uncover the clues that can lead to healing.

Here are the silent truths woven into the fabric of these stories:

The Unseen Struggles: Stories of resilience from us who carry heavy weights behind bright, everyday smiles.

The Quiet Miracles: Unearthing the profound, life-altering moments that happen in the shadows of the ordinary.

The Deep Connections: An exploration of the unspoken threads that bind us all, regardless of the different paths we walk.

Welcome to the collection. The pages that follow are a bridge between the visible and the invisible.

Introduction

For years, my stories lived in the digital ether, cataloged post by post. They began as solitary reflections—fleeting thoughts, raw memories, and deeply personal vignettes typed out in the quiet hours of the night. To the casual observer scrolling through a screen, these entries might have looked like scattered fragments. But to me, they were the road map of a much larger, internal expedition, and they became clues to my healing.

The Invisible Soul Anthology is the culmination of those digital footsteps brought into the physical reality of healing. Words are the reality that brings healing to every soul.

The phrase "The Invisible Soul" represents the parts of the human experience we so often hide from the world. It is the quiet resilience that keeps us moving forward when we are drowning in silent doubt, fear, or grief. For a long time, I wore a mask, hiding the unseen forces and internal whispers that dictated my choices and actions. Writing became my only tool for survival and self-exploration.

By pulling these stories from the archives of my library and organizing them into this anthology, I invite you to see what was once hidden in the shadows. Each story is a way-point on a long road toward emotional healing, raw truth, and ultimate redemption.

This anthology does not follow a straight, clinical timeline. Instead, it mirrors the natural ebb and flow of life itself. You will find:

The Whispers: Early reflections dealing with internal conflicts, unvoiced fears, and the heavy weight of expectations.

The Crossroads: Turning points where choices had to be made, masks had to be dropped, and truth had to be faced.

The Light: Stories of survival, spiritual grounding, and the quiet triumph of the human spirit over adversity.

You may choose to read this book from cover to cover, or you may open it to a random page whenever your own soul feels a bit too invisible to the rest of the world.

What started as personal therapy was never just about me. It was about finding a universal language for the invisible battles we all fight. By sharing my journey, my deepest hope is that you find pieces of your own story hidden within these pages.

Thank you for stepping off the digital screen and walking alongside me on this path. Welcome to *The Invisible Soul Anthology*. Healing With Words.

Life Line

I find it refreshing to be disconnected from social media, but I must admit I am connected more than I'm not. With all the noise on social media, it seems everyone has something to say, and while their words may be true, there are only so many ways to say something. It's exhausting at times to be so connected in this world.

Rarely do we hear someone say, "Help me." The point of this story is to encourage you to be vulnerable enough to ask for help when you need it. I understand how difficult it can be to reach out to others; it took a near *click* experience for me to say those words. I was so close to what I now call *the click*–the last sound you hear before death. Nearly 38,000 males commit suicide each year, which averages out to a man dying by suicide approximately every thirteen minutes. That's more than one hundred a day. *Let that sink in.* The pressure is intense out there. I'm just being honest. Some days, you just want to quit.

My transparency may be my enemy here, but I must write this story for what it is. This is the fourth start of this story. I have left the others in their place and have not changed them. They will speak for themselves as you read. I felt an urgency to write about transparency and how that plays a role in our healing. As we traveled home today from Southport, I realized I might have misled you in my writing to think that I am completely healed, whole, and perfect. I am far from that and still struggle daily with this awful unholy body that experiences the triggers that force me to be in places that I really don't want to be. Sometimes a conversation, a place of business, a restaurant, or even a certain smell can trigger feelings and memories of my past. Even a person's glasses or a reaction of a conversation can ignite an emotion that causes me to want to escape this world. It's real, and I haven't experienced healing for that. There is only secondary management to these symptoms of destruction. They are manageable, yes, and that's the wonderful news here. It may be a mystery now, but the hope in the end is there is victory.

As I sit on the edge of the Cape Fear River bank today in Southport, I realize there is less to life than it has been. Life is short. Each and every day that goes by, my focus funnels into this small lens of reality. Heading into this story, I wonder if this is my last one or will there be more? I have such an urge in my soul to write this one. I really don't want to because I know it's taking me places I don't want to go to and expend energy I don't want to expend. My soul wants to push forward, so we will do it together. Just me, my soul, and my spirit. Softly, we will travel this journey of death, destruction, and hopelessness. This has been a writing journey so far; night and day, I keep adding to this story.

There is so much to write here as they are all gone, and my soul is blessed to be still here. I'm still here! I'm coming off the last story, *Jenny,* which was so fun to write and full of love and beautiful endings. I'm not sure how this one came to life, but as with all my stories, they just happen at will. It seems all my stories may hold clues to my healing. I hope to put these clues together one day and see a beautiful ending. That day will come, and I feel it will be soon.

As we head into June, which is men's mental health month, I wanted to share a series of ominous stories with you all. They entail both past pains and present pains. This story includes several *red door* stories all at once and one that might become a red door story if I don't write it out now. I don't want to bury this present pain deep in my mind and lock it in my soul forever. In the past four years, I have learned how to unlock the clues of healing through stories and experiences I have been through. I am not singular in this journey; there are so many with me. I am not alone, and surely others are traveling with me now. Come and join me in this journey. I know you are here with me even now. I can feel you reading this story and know that I am speaking to those of you who are afraid to tell someone. Tell them! Tell them now! Speak what you need to say and let it be known that you need help to live before you become one of them.

I will name those that did not speak. There is my dad, Matthew, *click*. There is Tammy, *click*, who I was engaged to before I met my sweet Lisa. I truly loved Tammy. Then there was Tammy's mom, who was murdered. There is Kevin, *click*, and his wife Kathy, *click*. There is Kevin and Tammy's son, Matt, and there is my brother Chris. There are those who were in your circle but disappeared into the darkness and now don't exist in this world. There are those you have prayed for who have left this earth so unaware and quietly that even time itself has forgotten. Have we gotten so involved in our own social circles that we have missed them. Mine are just a handful of so many. Those whose tragic endings impacted many lives; some say they made the choice or the choice was made for them. By murder, by noose, the trigger, or jump, their decision was based on life choices before the event ever took place. Most say it was their choice, and I am going to strongly disagree. What happens to you, that which is invisible to the world, brings people to a point of no return most of the time. I want to write more about this one day and maybe I will. For now, we are going to move forward.

What happened to our hope, our purpose, and our calling? What happened?

A bullet, a noose, a jump, or even a plunge into a deep pit of overwhelming pressure took their joy and their lives because they could not say the words that they needed to say. *Hey, can you help me?* I was once in their shoes, and that's the most frightening part of writing this story. I wanted to quit. I wanted to be with them. I was one click away.

I had one desire and that was to be alone and leave a note for my family. I felt so alone, but on the outside, no one saw anything but a normal person full of joy and happiness. No one saw beyond the mask, and I made sure to never show my true feelings. For those who are hiding behind the mask, it's a show to the end. My voicemail would have sounded like this, "Hey, I just want you to know where to find me and know that I love you forever and ever. I adore you and with every breath I adored you. Know that my life was for you and for the girls. I love you, girls. I just couldn't continue any longer. It was too great and the pressure was too much. I'm so sorry to leave you this way. I love you." Then, *click*!

Now to the present. I made it! Yes, I made it. You can make it, too. No click, no noose, no plunge, no plan to exit. I am breathing a sigh of relief. I'm going to do my best to explain what's going on right now and what happened in the days that led up to this moment. But there is a twist to this story, and I want you to be ready for it as it will not end with all love and flowers. Here's the real story.

This all started about four and a half years ago. Death had approached my doorstep in the form of memories that were calling me to death. *It's time*, they said. *You can do this*. Night after night, I didn't even want to sleep anymore as the call was so ominous and intense. It was real to me. Just recalling it now makes me nervous about sleeping tonight. If you've been in a similar situation, you know what I'm talking about. It's a voice and voices that are never silent. They have but one goal and that is to destroy and kill. I told Lisa to hide the gun and never tell me where it was. It's still hidden to this day. You who are here reading this now know what I am saying. Let this story speak to you; let it rest in your soul and seek some help.

Suicide has been a strong voice in my life for many years; it was even whispered in my ears as a young child. In my formative years, there was no hope and the only answer was death. In the years that followed, only death could have brought peace to my troubled soul. It was an option to my soul. Then I decided enough was enough. and I would reach out to someone.

I made a call from work that day to a friend hoping she would help me. I hoped she would hear the urgency in my voice and she did. Ava is my friend but also a therapist. We agreed to meet the next week, and she said we had fifty-five minutes in the session; that was the only fifty-five-minute session we ever did.

From then on, our sessions were at least two hours to two and one half hours long. Ava often joked that on Mondays she cleared her appointments after 5:00 pm and didn't schedule much that day in general. Mondays were the day. I looked forward to them most of the time. They were exhausting but at the same time, relief came out of each session. Our conversations were in-depth and no boundaries were unexplored.

I explained what was going on and shared with her my past from age five to now. This is where I am now wanting to end it all. Her response was, "Do you have a plan? You know, a plan, the plan to end it all?" My response was a hard no, but she knew I had been thinking about what the outcome might be. Her response back to me was simple and true even to this day, "If you come up with a plan, please call me and let me know what that might be, and if you can't get me, call 988 right away." I smiled and started to nervously laugh. She was dead serious as she looked at me without smiling and with no expression on her face. She was letting me know the seriousness of my state of mind. Her urgency set the tone for each and every session.

She dug into the depths of my being and discovered things that were hidden and forgotten for all eternity. Ava is gifted as she had an unwavering way to dig down to bedrock and turn over stones that were so heavy that even I could not overturn them. There she would find the gold and every now and then a nugget. She was patient to share these findings and insert them in my mind in perfect timing. Often saying, "You know, George, or apparently George, you don't know. You keep doing the same thing over and over, thinking the same and enduring the same. There is a better way, let me share it with you."

I had hidden things so deep and didn't want to ever expose them to anyone. Lisa sat quietly with me at each session and discovered even more about me, even after forty years of marriage. Four years went on and each session brought new life to me and a new beginning to my life. I began a fresh journey and discovered a different pathway, full of meaning and purpose. I discovered a new way to deal with my pain, a new plan, and a new light to my path. The most important plan is having no plan to exit this life.

Therapy has ended for me now, not because I wanted it to but because circumstances changed. The tools Ava has given me will last a lifetime. She poured herself into my soul for four years, and I am forever grateful. I am now in what I call secondary management. Past the point of the *click* and now in the living for purpose.

Here's what secondary management looks like: it's evaluating every circumstance and deciding if I can sit here, stand here, be here, and see this. If not, what are the risks involved and is there a plan to escape? There is always an escape route in all circumstances. With this plan in place, I feel like I could take on the world. It's been now more than four and a half years with Ava. Am I healed? That is relevant only to the circumstance and how it evolves and what the outcome becomes. It's not perfect but very manageable now. My sweet Lisa plays a key role in all of this as well.

I have to take a break from this story for a few days now, and I will be back to it soon. I will remind my mind to come back quickly because time is of the essence, and I know there are those who are reading this whose lives may be in the balance.

I am now waking up at my scheduled time (3:30 am) each and every day to add to this story. I want to move forward now.

While in therapy on Sundays, I would receive a text just like the actual text below in this story; this took my life to a different place of pain, a caring that I never knew I had, a love that shattered all emotions, and to this day, am still processing. They read:

> December 31st - Lisa and I texted Ava
>
> Ava, Hope you had a great Christmas. Lisa and I wanted to wish you a Happy New Year.
>
> Response from Ava on January 1st.
>
> Happy New Year to you both!!! I had a pleasant Christmas with my son and daughter and grandkids! Then my oldest grandson drove me home so I did no driving on the way home. What a treat it was to have that special time together!

Text Received from Ava on January 11th.

Hi Lisa and George,

I was hospitalized last week at Rex Hospital in Raleigh where, after an MRI, the doctors found a brain tumor. They did a biopsy last Monday, and I will be heading to the Duke Brain Cancer Center next week with possible surgery soon. So, I won't be able to meet with you tomorrow. Also, if are interested, I can send your contact information for our therapy group. Let me know what you think will work best for you all. Had hoped to talk personally about this situation but it hasn't't been possible.

Ava

My Response:

Dear Ava,

We are so sorry to hear this news and quite honestly, we are completely devastated.

First and foremost, I want you to know we have prayed for you. You know I am never one to be lost for words but for now I am. I will do my best to convey my thoughts.

For more than four years now, we have received a text on

Sunday afternoon telling us we had an appointment with you tomorrow, and my response has always been, "Looking forward to our meeting." My response to Lisa has always been, "Don't have much to talk about." But that's never the case.

You have been instrumental in my healing journey, not only mentally but also in helping me discover and develop a creative side in a positive and empowering way. You have truly made a difference. For more than four years, you have made a meaningful impact on my life.

When we first met, I wanted to quit. But you turned that into a desire to change humanity. For that, I am forever thankful!

Lisa and I consider you a friend as well as a therapist! I know when we first started this journey you were not sure if it was possible to be a therapist and a genuine friend. But you soon found out that you could be both. It's not common in your industry but it worked.

We are so hopeful that healing will happen, and you will someday return to your couch. But if that doesn't happen, know that you have given us both powerful tools for life as we continue to navigate saving humanity. That should make you smile.

Now, as for reaching out to another therapist, you already know what I'm going to say. That's a no way, no how, not in this lifetime.

In my opinion, the last four years were designed by God Himself and for that we are forever grateful! Thank you, Ava, for your life-changing times, sessions, friendship, and most of all your presence!

We will be in contact with your daughter. We would love to see you if you are up to it, but we understand if you are not. We love you!!!

I have more news that will make you smile! I did finish writing *Lake Raleigh*. It's in edit. I will send it. It's my favorite of all time.

Sent Lake Raleigh Story January 16th

Response from Ava:

Love the story, George!!! It's wonderful that you can share how these places, people, and memories were healing back when you were small but still have the power to comfort you!

My Response to Ava January 17th:

Thank you, Ava, for your words. I did want you to know that you have been *Peanut* to so many in this life, leading them to a safe way out and to a new way!

For that, I am forever grateful! You have shaped and changed humanity, something that few do in this life.

Response from Ava January 19th:

So happy...I love how your words help your healing...I love the description as the safe *Peanut.* Happy to be that place for you.

Response again from Ava Monday January 19th:

I am thinking that if you print your stories while I am healing—when we meet, we can look them over together to see how they give clues on how best to continue your journey for healing and hope.

Words can never describe these texts with Ava back and forth. I've been thinking for months now how to convey this message and how these texts drifted through my soul. The one who introduced healing to me was now in dire straits. The one who now has an ending in sight is still wanting to meet with me, put the clues together, and see the journey through. That's an amazing and beautiful example of humanity.

So we're all done now? What happened and where did they go? This story may be the flagship of my existence. I want all who read this to know there is help for you; it doesn't have to end the way you are going. There is hope and there is healing. Healing takes a lifetime, and I am good with that as long as there is life in me. Ava helped me discover it was not my fault and the fault is not my justice to avenge. It's much bigger than that. This world needs you, and there is a purpose for you here.

If it sounds like I'm speaking to you who are on the edge of the bed with the gun in your hand, I am! If you are the one with the plan, please listen to me. If you are the one on the shore ready to take the plunge, then please listen to me. Stop and know you are more, and you didn't create this mess; you are so much more than this mess you are in. I've been right where you are. There is help. You just have to make that call you've been putting off. You have to send that text you been meaning to send, and you need to make that call to your trusted friend and just say it. *I need some help*.

Even though beauty comes from ashes, remember that even after the fact the ashes are still on the ground and still visible in life. The scars are deep and visible, but they are also invisible much of the time. The mental aspect of healing is just that—a journey of the soul as well as the mind. Book knowledge is valuable, but it's the willingness to dig deeper and uncover the fine gold and even the nuggets, that truly brings life to those who desperately need it. We should embrace life, love while we can love, and adore those in our lives; we are not promised tomorrow. Come on now, let's love this life together and make a way for this brokenness to be healed. Don't you quit! We need you here!

Let's do this for you, and let's do this for your family. Let's do this for humanity, ending this curse of destruction and death. Let's do this for the Avas who are here and the Avas who are to come. Make a difference and answer those who are speaking *help me*. Be a life line.

Tears

Lately, my tears have been flowing pretty freely. They could break through during a movie, a short film, a personal encounter, a story, or even a slight glance.

Sometimes it can be a curse to see pain as it exists in the present. Not all tears represent sadness, though. Over the last few years, I have learned that life contains beautiful moments of joy, happiness, and love. This should have been developed in my formative years, but those moments were spent in survival mode, figuring out the next hiding place or the next escape plan. So many tears were dropped in so many different places. Never to be found and lost in time.

I want this story to uncover and define the tears of joy and the joy of sadness. The tears seem to come from the same aqueduct but from different regions of our hearts. That's what makes this story both complex and simple at the same time.

I spent most of my life fighting tears as if they were the enemy. I still fight them from time to time. The older I get, the more I lose this battle. Tears can jump out of my eyes in an instant.

While I write, I usually play music in the background. I'm writing this story in my office, which also houses about four hundred vintage records. One of my favorites is playing right now, and it is speaking so loudly to me that I have to share it with you. I remember hearing this song for the first time when it was released in nineteen seventy-four, and it became my theme song; it describes my life as it was then. I encourage you to go and listen to it now. It's called *Haven't Got Time for the Pain* by Carley Simon, and it's about moving past heartbreak and emotional struggles and choosing to focus on healing rather than dwelling on the hurt. It emphasizes letting go of the pain and not letting it take up space in your life.

The pain I didn't have time for then was buried deep in my soul, and I promised never to visit it or even shed a tear for it. It didn't deserve the time or effort, as it had one goal, and that was to destroy me. I know we all have these memories, no matter how we grew up or what we encountered in life. We have a pain that we decided never to have the time for. This was my coping mechanism, and I believe it's true for most of us.

Turns out, some sixty years later, I had to find time for the pain, or it was going to end my life. This pain surfaced with a vengeance, and I didn't know what to do with it. The tears flowed deep into the night, screaming unbearably in my mind. It became a voice in my life and started to control me. It would surface at any time; a simple grocery store or gas station visit would send me over the edge. My heart would start to pound, and I looked for a way out.

Lisa, my sweet wife of forty years, sensed something was surfacing, and she knew it might be bigger than both of us. She has always had this second sense of my inner being and how it speaks. Her persistent question to me is always, "Are you ok?" She speaks her concern in the softest voice you could ever imagine. She follows with, "How can I help you?" Even today, she said, "I am here; I will shield you. I'm here for you." She sees the struggle in my eyes, which opens a pathway to my pain, the gateway to my soul.

One of the primary ways I've dealt with pain in the past is to separate from anything or anyone who causes it. It was so simple back then, and even now, I find myself falling back into that way of thinking. If it causes pain and tears, then I want to separate from it. Be it a story or a relationship, I end it and cut it off. No matter the cost, it has to go.

Over the last four years, I have learned that this is not a healthy way to deal with pain. The tears are still there, and these voices still seek to build a front and destroy. I believe I've made enormous progress over the last four years by learning to deal with pain; now my tears are turning from pain to joy. The tears flow from the joy of the relationships with friends and family. The healing in so many areas of my life has changed me. With every victory, there seems to be a counter to the pain that surfaces.

The tears are recognized by what's encapsulated in them. Every tear has a purpose. Some have the purpose of joy, and some have a purpose of pain release. You have to look at each tear that is released and question it. Why this tear? Look at it and discover the origin and the purpose, and then discover the extraordinary healing that tears can bring. Tears are like writers; they are storytellers.

If I haven't said it yet in a way you can understand, your tears can lead you to death, or they can bring overwhelming joy to you. Your tears can bring your pain to the surface; it's an opportunity to discover healing. There is one key element to this whole process: be willing to go down that path.

The tears of joy are radiant and spontaneous, a sacred release of memories once held or new ones being formed. If placed under a microscope, they would shimmer with the language of love, mercy, and grace. These tears have the power to bring you to your knees, stirring a depth of emotion that words cannot explain. For so long, I've lived without them. Now they come quietly, mostly from moments with family members or through simple conversations of victory. Yes, the victories encountered over the last few years have brought these tears to existence. There is a river within me now, no longer held back and flowing freely without restraint.

There is an old saying: "Your past colors your future." I believe that now, but we still have the power to choose the colors and how they are expressed. The tears of pain and suffering will rise; they are raw, unfiltered, and at times overwhelming. They demand to be acknowledged and not hidden deep in our souls. These tears are a raging river, carrying the weight of our most difficult seasons—the places where sin once took root, where wounds were inflicted, where we faltered, and where we were broken. It's where torture took place, and it's where death called us, but we didn't answer.

These tears of death are extremely heavy in so many lives today. Seek help from a friend, a spouse, a family member, or even a stranger who will listen.

Tears are transparent, and when they are seen, they desire a response. Never be so busy that you bypass the opportunity to jump in and join the river of joy or the river of sadness. Both bring healing. Tears are telling a story of His amazing grace. Once lost but now found. Find time for the pain, or it will find your time.

Jenny

So, what's in a name? How can you unpack and write a story about just a name? It's been in my mind for months now, even before the last story. This one was supposed to come out before that one, but for some reason, it was delayed.

As with most of my stories, they are written in my mind and then brought to life through my fingertips on this virtual piece of paper. I could only imagine writing this with pen and paper or on a real type writer. This story is so different, and it has evolved in my mind with only two words: *friendship* and *Jenny*. More than anything, I want to honor both of them. There is one hindrance in this story and that is time.

It's been forty years since I've seen Jenny or even spoken to her, but her presence in my life was so impactful during the years we spent together. As I mentioned early on, this story has no direction as of yet, but I will do my best to paint a picture with words that illustrate how gratitude, love, and the presence of a beautiful soul can help steer the course of one's life.

Just yesterday, Lisa was asking me about my next story. I told her that I would like to write about Jenny. She had the opportunity to meet her back then. At this moment, I can feel the emotional tears rising up from deep in my soul as I recall this precious friendship. Friendships never die; they just linger in the background ever so lightly with a memory or a spot in time that changed us somehow. Jenny was the person; she was that friend.

She didn't know it then, but she played a pivotal role in bringing me out of an extremely dark time. She never dug too deep, never adjusted herself to accommodate me, and looked at me for who I was. I gave her the same respect back. Let me see if I can paint this picture for you.

Forty years ago, before I met my sweet Lisa, I was a person full of pain and dealing with so much suffering from the trauma and torture I had come out of. Then there was Jenny. She had moved into the apartment across the hall from me. I had just finished trade school and had my first blue collar job as an auto mechanic at a local dealership. This is the same dealership where I met my sweet Lisa at as well.

Right now, I am taking a moment to reflect on how much joy this story is bringing me; I see the gratitude, love, and presence of her friendship. I can visualize her face across the hall as she introduced herself for the first time. One word describes her presence: acceptance! As tears flow down the cheeks of my face, I can remember her smile and feel the love she has for humanity. Who was she? We became, in my mind, the best of friends.

We spent the weekdays and weekends together, traveling and enjoying everything life had to offer. It was not uncommon for us to be at a concert on a Friday night and then at a steeple chase race the next day. She introduced me to culture, for which I am forever grateful. I think that's part of this story and how it evolved. I was watching a horse race with Lisa recently, and I described a moment when Jenny and I had attended a steeple chase race here in North Carolina. I would be amiss not to mention Anna who completed this trio. She brought a balance to the group.

Jenny had asked if I wanted to go to the horse race, a steeple chase. I had no idea what she was talking about, but since it meant spending time with her, I was in. This is how I remember the event.

We came out in the apartment hallway at about the same time; she was wearing a beautiful colored dress and holding a vibrant hat. I was in shorts and a tee shirt. She gave me the *up and down* look and spoke with her eyes. I went back into my apartment and returned in blue jeans and a button-down oxford shirt. She nodded with approval and we jumped in her car and drove away. No words. Her eyes could speak words that never needed to be spoken.

Looking back, we adored our time together. We loved the time, the places, and the moments as if they were meant for healing. Every breath and every life experience with Jenny brought refreshment to my soul; you have to fill in the blank here.

My soul was so injured in those times, and she seemed unaware at the time, even though I now know she always knew. That's why our relationship was so beautiful. She knew, and she was accepting of the gratitude and the love, and she gave her presence to me. Who could ever ask for a friend like Jenny?

I was not worthy of her presence on most days, but looking back now some forty years later, she led me to my next journey, my sweet Lisa. Who, by the wonderful grace of God, accepted my friendship with Jenny as a wonderful part of my memory bank that I can access from time to time. As I sit here writing this now, I can see how much I adored Jenny.

Oh, my soul was blessed by our friendship. It was a time of change, a time of giving, and a time of peace in my soul. Jenny brought life to me, but she didn't know. Jenny brought promise to me, but she never knew. Jenny brought a new beginning to me, but she never knew. She lifted me high and brought life to a soul that was so wounded that only God knew what I needed at that time.

I will leave you with this as tears flow down my face once again, my soul is blessed by my remarkable friendship with Jenny. Never take for granted those in your life now and those that are to come. There is a greater purpose in the works. Follow them, and be grateful for those relationships in your life both past present and future.

Jenny, thank you! If I never see you again or connect with you again, know that our time together was more than friendship. It was full of grace, gratitude, love, and mostly your presence in my life to make me a better person, preparing me for the next journey.

If time allows and fate happens, then these are my words to you, Jenny.

A note to Jenny: I made it! We made it! Lisa and I made it. We raised two beautiful girls, Sara and Laura. We have five amazing grandsons and two beautiful sons-in-love. I'm still here. Thank you for the time you spent with me and invested in our lives together, never expecting anything in return. I love you, Jenny! You are a wonderful friend who has blessed my soul with life.

Be mindful of the friendships that come into your life. They have a purpose, so adore each and every one of them. They are all part of the journey of gratitude, love, and presence which equals purpose. Purpose brings life.

Grace Given! Grace Received!

"Is that what we can expect today?"

Those words shouted from the boat that day were a reminder of the grace we are given every day. It makes me wonder if God is sitting on the throne of Grace and asking, "Is that what I can expect today?" Let me give you the back story. I will do my best to explain.

I was an avid water skier just a few short years ago. I entered the sport very late in life, but I became addicted to every aspect of it. The first time the girls and I skied on the course was at a local ski club close to our house.

John became a close friend who invited us to give it a try there; he was a member of the club. Even though we thought we skied great, we were at a beginner level. I asked John, "What did you think of our skiing?" He said, "The girls did well, but your skiing is probably some of the ugliest skiing I've ever seen." His comment didn't deter me; I was fully committed to the sport. We joined the ski club, and over the years, our skiing improved significantly. We started to compete in local competitions. Waterskiing became part of our family, and the waterski community became part of our family as well. As with all sports, if you want to get better, you have to invest in coaching.

During that time, a weekend-long waterski clinic was being held near us, a couple of hours away in Greenville, NC. Two of my waterski idols were coaching—Kristi Overton and Jeff Rodgers. All you had to do was call the number and register. Laura, our youngest daughter, and I really wanted to go. Sara didn't express an interest in going: she just enjoyed the sport.

I called the number, and I was a bit shaken when Kristi answered. I was so nervous after finding out who it was. She said she would love to have us there and explained the clinic's cost. She must have heard the distress in my voice when she explained the cost. I told her I would do my best to raise funds so I could make it. Just a few minutes later, she called back. She said, "I really want you to be able to make it, so plan on coming and just pay what you can, no worries; it will be fun." Grace given! Grace received!

I was the only one who was going to get coaching; Laura came along with me to cheer me on. I told her to watch and learn as much as she could from the shore, and I would teach her everything I learned when we returned to the ski club. We met up at Lake Kristi early that morning, and the fog was slowly lifting off the water as the boat rumbled in the background. I know, and yes, the lady has her own lake, and that's another story in itself. Laura and I were standing on the shore. I had my ski, gloves, and handle. There was a group of about ten skiers. We talked about skiing stuff mostly.

In the distance, I saw a tall figure coming up the hill, and beside him was a kid on a small motorcycle. Someone in the crowd whispered, "That's Jeff Rodgers." I almost fell out from excitement. He was my all-time hero in waterskiing. He came over to the group and talked for only a few moments; he is a man of few words. His son was sitting close by on his motorcycle, enjoying his father's time. Laura and I stood off to the side of the group, amazed at the waterskiing legend. Then Kristi drove up on a golf cart with her dad, Parker. We just stared at them awkwardly. Now we call that the *goofy stare.*

Parker approached Laura and me and asked if we were both skiing. Laura said, "No, just my daddy." He asked, "Where is your ski?" She said, "In the car." He asked her to get in the golf cart and later returned with her and her ski, gloves, and handle. "She's skiing this weekend, too," he said. Grace given! Grace received!

I could write an entire book on this family and what they have done for my family. This was a brief encounter with them, and in the years to come, life-changing experiences would take place because of them. I believe we crossed paths for a reason, and I thank God that He brought them into our lives.

Now back to the lake. I continued to stare at my idol, Jeff Rodgers, and he said, "Who's first up today?" Thankfully, someone spoke up and said they would go. I was trying to hide in the crowd because I was so nervous. They skied and seemed to do well. As the boat pulled back up to the shore, a voice from the boat said, "George." I was shaking but ready to learn from one of the best.

I climbed onto the platform and put on my ski and gloves. Jeff said, "Just relax and have fun." I was thinking, *Have fun? 'Cause I'm here to tear this course up. I'm about to show you something.* I dropped into the water, and the boat rounded the turn island, and then I started my glide out to get ready to enter the course. I had pulled so hard that I got into what is called a *lean lock,* hit some ripples in the water, and then fell before I ever entered the course.

Who gets lean locked pulling out for the glide? I thought as I slowly rose from under the water. Everyone on the shore was staring at me as the boat pulled back over to me. Then Jeff stood up tall in the boat, slowly brought the ropes back in, and simply said, "Is that what we can expect today? I mean, really, is that it?" Then gave me one of the biggest and most comforting Jeff Rodgers' smiles I have ever seen. Later in this life, I would learn that that is who he is. Grace given! Grace received!

After that failed first attempt, I learned so much that I skied the best I had ever skied. Even to this day. I received.

So many positive things came out of the meetings that weekend; it was never about waterskiing. There is and was a much larger purpose in those times. That's for a whole book that I hope to write someday. There were experiences all over the United States of America that not only changed my life, but also those of many others, not because of me, but those who chose to share grace.

The heart of this story is about grace given and grace received. In my life, there has been so much grace given. Have I received all that has been offered? Probably not. Why not? That's the whole point of the story right now.

To the addict, the lost, and the homeless. To the struggling marriage and to the one who wants to quit today—give grace. When I wanted to quit, grace was given; when my marriage wasn't what it should have been, grace was given; when I felt less than, grace was given; and when I fell, grace was given.

It's up to you to receive the grace that is given. Never be so busy or so important in your own eyes that you can't give grace. Those I met that day gave amazing grace and changed so many lives. Stand up tall in the midst of it all, smile, and know you're going to be okay. Receive grace! Give grace!

The undercurrent of all of this, and the thing that took me months to put into words, is that *the most amazing grace is the grace of Jesus Christ.*

Receive that grace today!

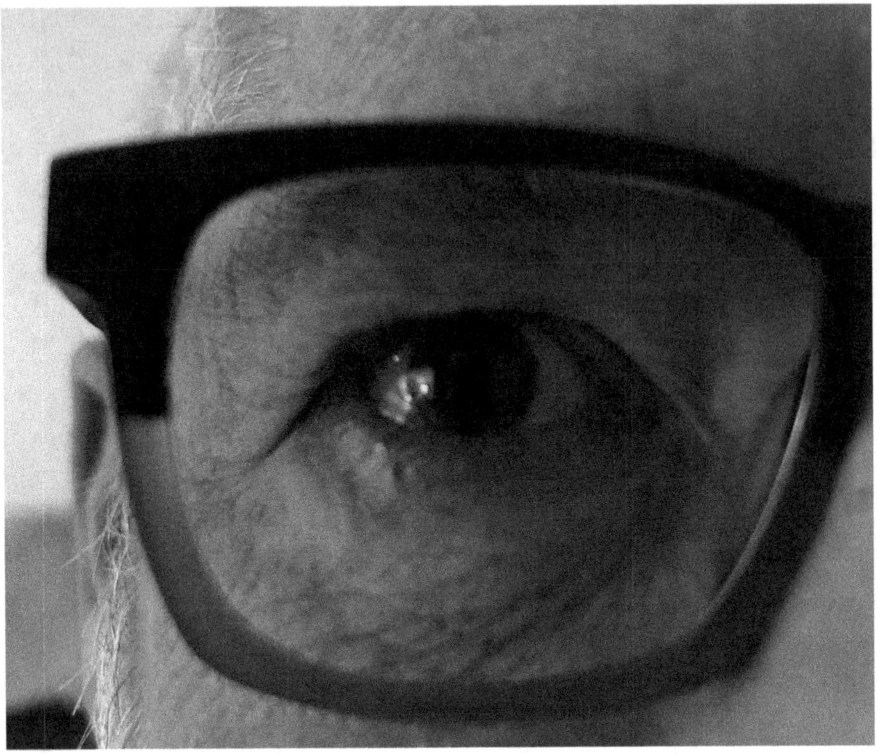

The Lens

So many words are spoken today, and so much background noise fills the air, creating confusion. Future generations will not stand a chance unless we begin to speak truth through the lens of wisdom, the lens of experience, the lens of reality, and above all, through the lens of love and truth.

The older I get, the more clearly my lens focuses on what truly matters—the real meaning of life—and the powerful truth that it's never too late to shape humanity through words.

We have to help the next generation turn away from their addiction to knowledge, their addiction to social platforms, and their addiction to fame. Our minds were never meant to absorb so much information, and this has caused our lenses to become blurred far too early in life.

We may not bring anything new to the table, but what we do have is a more focused lens—sharpened by years, pain, and perspective—unlike the generations coming behind us. We now compete with machines that have fostered a deep addiction to information, shaping the lenses of humanity across all ages. Just look around the next time you are out and see humanity with their heads down and their eyes locked on their machines.

The lens will tell the real story. A focused lens reveals the truth, but if it's distorted, it brings lies into reality. I have looked through the lens as a twenty-year-old, as a thirty-year-old, as a forty-year-old, as a fifty-year-old, and now as a sixty-year-old. I now see more clearly the traumas that have shaped me. I have accepted the fact that I was not the cause but a casualty of a lens that was so blurred and full of evil. As I walked into the path of that evil lens, nothing but torture took place. I tried my best to stay out of sight.

Those traumas have given me a unique vision, a hard-earned clarity that helps me fight my battles one at a time—mostly with myself, and sometimes with those around me. Some never realize they are in the focus of my lens. They are just stray casualties of the ever-changing lens and the unwanted focus that was not meant for them. They take it personally, but it's not that way at all. The fact of the matter is that what comes into the view of the lens has a purpose, and that purpose is to bring a clear vision to our humanity, our life, our purpose, and our existential being.

I have come to one conclusion about this story. It is much more complex than just a short one-liner. With that said, I will focus on what's ahead.

It's been weeks now, and I'm still struggling with the direction. The front end of this story has changed so many times. I believe it's because when we sit back and take time to bring clarity into focus, the lens brings something that is so beautiful that we can say, *That's it!*

That's what's different about my twenty-year-old lens, my thirty-year-old lens, and even my forty-year-old lens. These years were about taking everything in and processing what came into focus. My formative years were so blurry. I lived in survival mode, where there was no time to focus on anything else.

I know that's not the case for all of humanity. I often wonder what it's like to be looking through a twenty-year-old lens right now; it must be terrifying. Even the thirty and forty-year-old lens must carry deep concern for what's to come.

But a focused lens brings hope and a calm reality. We all come from uniquely shaped lenses, and that's what makes this world so beautiful and diverse. If we all shared the same focus and the same lens in this life, we would not need *Him*. That's the beauty of the lens; it builds us, layer by layer, shaping us through the years.

Now, my fifty-year-old lens was the start of a revolution inside of my soul. I'm not sure if that's true for all lenses that develop in our humanity, but for me, it sparked a new clarity. To be honest, the late fifties brought an awakening of sorts that led me into a new era. I realized that I had spent so many years running from the very clarity that I was searching for. I kept the focus I desired out of reach because of fear. I was afraid of what would come into view, afraid of what clarity might bring. I fought hard. And now, I am in my sixty-year-old lens.

I am still fighting for clarity. I want to see, but I am still fearful of this past that seems to emerge with new memories and destruction. Yet I now have tools—handed to me by the grace of beautiful people who were placed in my life.

Despite all the scratches, rough spots, and blurred areas on my lens, there is hope. The scratches are reminders of past losses and past victories—each one now clearer in hindsight. The rough patches reflect the mountains I have climbed and the roads I have traveled. The blurred spots? Maybe they're just meant to stay there for now. Maybe that's grace, too.

No matter where you are in your lens of life, accept the scratches, the rough patches, and even the blur. These are all part of the journey. Look at what's in focus now. Work on that. That's where you are right now. That's what matters.

Clarity will come with time. Don't rush toward it so quickly that you miss the understanding meant for the moment. True clarity will never come from the machines designed to overwhelm our minds. It comes through genuine connection—one-on-one—and through alignment with our purpose in life.

Our relational response to one another is what brings clarity and vision to our purpose in life.

So, let's continue to polish our lenses—the lens of compassion, attention, purpose, and love.

The Sandbar

From time-to-time, memories surface that I don't understand how to express, much less write about. This is one of those rare memories that was triggered by the last story, *Jane.*

A river, flowing just down the street from our trailer, became part of our daily lives. It wasn't a particularly powerful river, but graceful, lofty trees lined its banks and provided us shade and a place of solace. These trees had been drinking out of the river for centuries. They spoke so many stories to us, of those who had been before us, and of those who would follow.

This was during a time that I happened to be at home—what I described in the last story as a *rest stop* for me. The principals at my current residence were playing well and showed no signs of torture, but I knew that was just a matter of time.

On any hot summer day, my brothers, Mike and Chris, would join me down by the river. Jane would come with us as well; she wasn't much into fishing but enjoyed the time we spent together.

We had a special place where we fished—it was called the sandbar. It appeared mostly when the river was at its lowest. I remember us walking through the trailer park, fishing poles in hand, heading down the street to that path in the woods—the one that led to our special spot on the river. We were excited to see that sandbar as we stepped over the puddles of water and made our way onto that exquisite place. We kicked off our shoes as soon as we reached the sandbar, and the sand felt coarse on our bare feet. Our toes sunk into the sand, and we felt the wonder of God's creation. This place gave us a glimpse of who God was, even though we didn't know much about God at that point; we were mostly in survival mode. One thing we knew for sure—the sandbar led us to a place of hope and peace.

The sandbar served several purposes, and one was to give us the perfect spot to cast our lines across the river to the large rock on the other side—where all the hefty catfish lay. When the river was high, that rock was out of reach, but when the river receded and the sandbar emerged, we had access to those massive cats.

The expansive sandbar contained both sun and shade. Fresh beams of sunlight shined overhead, and shade was in abundance as well.

Jane wrote in the sand most of the time; she often would play a game and ask, "What did I spell?" I always took time to answer regardless of the intense fishing going on.

We were all in place but yet out of place on the sandbar. The grace the sandbar brought us also brought us more beauty than we could have ever imagined. Here's that one memory I have.

First I tied on the bolts and nuts to my fishing line, added some old stinking chicken livers to my hook, and cast over to the big rock. The line hit bottom, and I set my pole in the sand; the pole rested on a fork of a branch I had set just under the first eyelet on the pole. Then I waited. We watched all the poles that were set, waiting as the river pulled the lines ever so lightly. Suddenly, my pole went from a straight position to almost touching the water of the river. I grabbed the pole quickly and started to reel. I screamed, "It's a big one; it's a big one. My friends ran over to me, and Mike and Chris encouraged me to keep reeling. They were screaming, "Reel, reel; you got 'em." The fight went on for what seemed like hours, but it was just minutes. We just wanted to see that monster! What was it? Was it the big one we had always dreamed of catching?

I kept reeling, and finally, he surfaced right in front of us all; we were eye to eye with this enormous fish. I stopped reeling and walked backward, dragging him on the sandbar. He had to be three feet long. We were not much taller than he was. He was now completely out of place, but we needed to show him off to the trailer park. Otherwise, no one would have believed us.

I can vividly remember us all, including Jane, jumping for joy and feeling ecstatic the moment we caught that massive fish. There was never any question about what we were going to do with him—it was unspoken. I grabbed him by the gills, and we headed to the trailer. It was a struggle to get to our destination. Once we entered the house, my brother Mike instantly started filling the bathtub with water. That's right, we put that fish right in the tub. He seemed happy, but we all knew he was out of place.

As the fish filled the entire tub, we summoned all our friends in the trailer park; it was like a sideshow of sorts. As the kids walked through our trailer to our bathroom, amazed by this anomaly of nature, we felt like the kings of the river.

Then the inevitable happened. Mom came home and flipped the trailer upside down. "Get that fish out of here. You can't keep him here. Take him back to the river where he belongs. He's out of place here!"

She actually took it way better than we thought. We laughed all the way back to the river. Jane reminded us that our laughter would soon end because of the look on our mom's face. Then we broke out crying with laughter all over again.

Back at the sandbar where our journey began, we laid him near the water, his head just touching the surface. As quickly as we pulled him in, he eased back into the water. He swam along the bank of the sandbar as if to thank us for putting him back into his place. Then, all of a sudden, he disappeared—back to the big rock to tell his story to all those who had witnessed his displacement. If only fish could talk. He was back where he belonged.

Being out of place can bring about pain, suffering, and even death. Being out of place can also bring new life, beautiful endings, and fresh beginnings. We were out of place on that sandbar, and yet, it led us to new places and brought us solace and peace at a time when we had no way to escape. As a family, we often seemed out of place—unwanted and in the way of others' stories. We survived in so many different places, either together or apart, but our family bond always remained strong.

This story has so many possible endings. I've been sitting on it for weeks now, pondering the perfect conclusion. I've even woken up at two and three in the morning, asking myself how it should end.

Being out of place is different for all of us. It can happen in a restaurant, a store, during a conversation, with a glance, a word, a smile, in a relationship, and even with family.

In the end, you only have to ask two questions when you feel out of place: "How do I get back? How do I return, healthy and ready to continue my story as it's intended to be written?"

So, what's your plan? You've got to get back! No matter what, you have to find your way back to where you belong.

Lake Raleigh

This story comes out of a vault from some fifty-plus years ago. If you have followed any of my stories, you know that when I call this a green door story, it's safe for me to write. A green door story is just that; it requires some energy, emotions, and self-examination. In other words, it's a story that is fun and a journey back in time.

The yellow door and red door stories require so much more of my heart, and those seem to be off limits to my fingers for right now. Being in therapy now for more than four years, I can tell you that tremendous progress has been made. I have written one red door story and many yellow door stories. So why are we recapping this as we start to write this story?

This is the first story I've written that parallels right alongside a red door story, and I am treading on a very thin rope that could snap at any time and tumble me into this unwritable experience. For that reason, I will start the narrative beginning with the bike ride to Lake Raleigh. The place I came from was nothing more than a din of torture for my siblings and me. If I go back one frame before this bike ride—one step off this bike and one fall in the wrong direction—I see nothing but torture, darkness, and pain. a time when life had ended for me. Now, let's see if we can do this.

On the hot summer days, we gathered together with our friend Phil, my brother Mike, and my brother Chris, who is no longer with us to recount this wonderful memory. He loved to fish. You already know he died at the age of thirty-seven from an overdose. He could never run fast enough from the pain. Chris would have loved this memory. My brother Mike and I have talked about this story recently. Sometimes he remembers facts that I have forgotten.

The lake wasn't that far from where we lived, so we all would either ride our bikes or walk. When you are young, a few miles isn't that far. Our path led down a couple of side streets and then to Lake Raleigh Road. It was a dirt road with some gravel spread on it in places. The road was winding and covered with a canopy of trees, not letting too much sunlight in. It was truly a road that was less traveled by any souls other than us. We had our fishing poles and maybe a hook or two. We found our bait under large rocks on the banks of the stream just below this massive dam. I say massive because at that age, this was the only dam we had ever seen.

There was a large pipe at the base of the dam that had a giant valve on it, some kind of a release of sorts. This pipe had a hole in it, and it sprayed water to the center of the stream we fished in. The dam was old, and now I know it was built in the early 1900s. Water always flowed over it ever so slightly, and it had a smooth finish. It was dark in color and made a peaceful sound that seemed to silence the troubles of that day. It kept promises to us every time we came there. The promise to love us and accept us at its base, no matter what we had experienced and what was to come. It never judged but was a savior to us all.

This place was so enchanting, calming, and tranquil, and it brought love to our troubled souls. We laughed at stories we recounted over and over. This place was a haven for us all. Our troubles didn't exist there; the darkness was empty there, and the evil was not allowed in that place. We made sure never to talk about what was going on just a few miles away. There was no way we would ever allow these conversations to happen.

The dam had its own folklore. According to legend, if you went to the top to fish, you had to be careful not to fall in. Catfish as big as Volkswagens lurked near the bottom, ready to swallow anyone who fell, and they would never be seen again. We respected that place, and in return, it gave us life. From time to time, we would venture up to the top, cast a line out, and then run back down the hill to our safe spot, laughing along the way. It was always a dare to see who would stay the longest.

We followed the stream, fishing the whole way and gathering bait and fish along the way. Someone would yell, "Got one," and "Got another one." On and on the day would go. At dusk, we knew we had to be out of there. There was another tale that said if you stayed after dark, bad things took place there, so we always headed out when the sun was setting.

One day, we found ourselves near the catfish pond, which was close to the creek. It was turning dark, and we were trapped. We saw a caravan of cars coming in from the back side of Lake Raleigh, and we were scared. Our hearts pounded with fear, and we needed a plan to escape, or else we were going to die. We lay on the bank, peering over toward those cars winding down that dirt road, kicking up dust. Then all of a sudden, a voice behind us yelled, "What y'all boys doing?" We turned ever so slowly, and it was our friend *Peanut* who had permitted us to fish in the catfish pond the summer before. "Peanut, we just want to go home." Did you catch that? We wanted to go home. Back to the place that meant pain, suffering, and yes, new tortures, but it was still home. I know it doesn't make sense, but we wanted to go home!

I don't even understand it to this day. The word *home* meant family; it meant there were times of some togetherness. It's where our mother was. The one who was supposed to protect us but failed immensely! I'm getting so close to that red door now, so we'd best move on. I'm about to unload on this whole situation.

Peanut would visit us at the catfish pond from time to time and was a savior of sorts, a friend indeed. After he saw the fright in our eyes that evening, he said, "Come with me, I'll show you the way out." We followed him on foot, pushing our bikes up the hill and down a road that was less traveled, and he guided us safely back. He pointed us in the right direction, and I still remember that to this day. It was the safe way. You always have to have a safe way back; never give up!

Now, some fifty years later, Lisa and I were riding around, and she said, "Where do you want to go today?" I said, "Lake Raleigh. I want to go to the dam today." She had heard some stories from this place, but I wanted to go deeper and finally write about it. She put it in the GPS, and we followed the directions. As we approached, I saw Lake Raleigh Road on the screen. My heart froze for a moment in time as it all flashed before me. To my right, nothing but destruction, and to my left, Lake Raleigh Road, peace and harmony. A gift that gave me life; it gave us all life.

The GPS said, "Turn here," but it was not Lake Raleigh Road; it was the road less traveled. It was the road out back then; it was the road right before where I thought we were supposed to turn. But wait, Lake Raleigh Road was now a dead end. How could it be? There is now a new way in, a new way around. As we entered this new road, I wondered if we would be able to get to the dam and if the stream would still be there. As we traveled this new way in, I could see the old way. Why was this, I wondered.

We went down one road and then another and another. I was trying to find this place on my own. When I finally listened to the GPS, it took me right to the place I remembered, Lake Raleigh. I saw the dam from a distance, and Lisa said, "Why are you in such a hurry?"

"I want to see that place one more time," I said. "I have to see it. Can we even get there from here?" It had changed so much over the years. There were people and places there that didn't exist back then. As we kept walking on the paved trail, I saw the dam. We headed off-grid to get there, and then there it was. WOW!

My heart filled with overflowing love and thankfulness for that place. I even whispered, "Thank you! Thank you for providing me with a safe haven in this place. I feel you working in this place even now." I walked down the stream a few hundred yards, recounting all the memories flooding in my soul, and a rush of light in the darkness reminded me of who God is.

As I looked up at the dam, I noticed it had changed. The water running down the face of the dam now made a new, soothing sound. Its appearance had transformed as well. The pipe is gone, and the sound it makes today is truly distinct.

The dam was rebuilt in 1976, giving it a fresh beginning, while maintaining its original purpose: to hold back water, provide those downstream with cherished memories, and serve as a reserve of drinking water for life. A new beginning, a fresh start, and a place that brings life to all who encounter it. Even today, you can follow the stream to reach your destination, and you may encounter Peanut, who will guide you to safety on a road less traveled. You understand. Then, when you return some fifty years later, you will see—you can do it! Don't quit!

This story has produced many more tears than I had ever expected. I didn't see it coming. Remember, God never stops moving. He is still doing it! Trust His road.

The River

Every river has an undercurrent that seeks to pull you down and destroy your life. It's called the undertow, or undercurrent. It's taken me seventeen years to bring this story from being buried deep within to the surface.

It was a beautiful sunny day, not too hot and not too cool. *Just right* some would say. The cookout was in full swing, honoring those who would serve the whole summer in an endeavor that would surely change lives for generations to come.

The undercurrent of the river could not be seen; it was a slow flowing river that seemed to be beautiful on the surface. Evil was lurking just below its calm exterior.

The Meramec River, or more commonly known as the *river of death*, was deceptively dangerous. As some waded out into the water, laughter cried out, and it was a joyful occasion. It was beautiful but there was an undercurrent that day that no one saw coming. As more people waded out into the river because the current looked so calm, the river was not speaking anything but peace and harmony in the moment. Then suddenly the undercurrent took over!

My voicemail to this day says, "George, give me a call; give me a call, there has been a tragedy." It was about two in the morning, and I was out of a cell service area. The next morning I arose early and went to a location where I could get a cell signal and made the call.

My friend answered with urgency and told me what had happened. "They died; they all drowned, five of them, George."

I didn't know what to say, other than "Why did God allow this?"

She said, "God didn't; the devil has orchestrated this evil."

The undercurrent had pulled them under, dragging them to the bottom of this godforsaken river—a river that had claimed lives before and would surely do so again. All five of them left a profound impact, altering the course of those they left behind in their wake. I was one of the few directly affected, swept up in the aftermath. The impact of their loss changed the course of my life forever, as it did for everyone involved in this tragedy. The undercurrent not only pulled them under but also left the living broken and haunted. That dam river! I hate that river. And I hate even more that it's taken me seventeen years to finally write about it.

I have always referred to them as *the five*—five souls who brought so much life to this world and had so much to share with humanity. Who would ever know now? The river of death claimed them,and now where are we? Living...but are we? What has the undercurrent done to us, the ones left behind? As I sat on the shore of the lake, I stared blankly into the horizon—a lost soul looking for direction, asking God, *Why? What happened? Why didn't you see this coming?* I was angry! *If you are God, then why did You allow this?* My questions seemed valid I thought, but they required no response from my God who created me and who holds the universe in His hands.

My soul sank to a new depth. Death could have received me in that moment, and I am sure I was not the only one who felt that way.

That was supposed to be the greatest summer of all times. We had planned to reach out to so many wonderful inner-city kids who had never seen the breathtaking nature of a lake, been on a boat, or even tried water skiing. Then the undercurrent happened. The evil that it holds, and the slow, unseen current beneath the surface, are always present. This undercurrent seeks to destroy us all.

At that time in my life, I truly wanted to disappear. It wasn't entirely about me or even this event, but something had shifted profoundly, leaving me with a deep, desperate wish to no longer be on this earth. The undertow is real. It doesn't just destroy those caught directly in its grip; it pulls at anyone near its edge, gradually drawing them in without their even realizing it. Suddenly, they're struggling to stay upright as it pulls them under.

A particular song resonated so deeply with me that I clung to it, and it sparked a shift in the *neighborhood* between my ears.

Linkin Park's *Numb,* captured exactly what I was feeling—a sense of being overwhelmed, weighed down by pressures beyond my control, and gradually becoming numb to everything around me.

I had become numb to the emotions causing me such intense pain. This is the point where you realize you're in a dark place, with the undertow threatening to engulf you into the phantoms of death.

This is the place where so many struggle to survive, where suicide can feel like the only escape from the unbearable pain. It's a place where your smile, your laughter, and even your words can hide what's really happening in your soul. You don't know the power of the undertow until it pulls you down and holds you there. It's dark and lonely, even with friends and family nearby. The undertow is where we all struggle to become more like Him, calling on Him with everything we have.

In the undertow, we feel numb but long for life. At rock bottom, hope feels lost, and in that place of despair, we cry out for something—anything—to bring us back to the light.

Then it happens. Hope shows up. It might come from a trusted friend, a daughter or son, a coworker, or even a stranger who has seen your struggle and offers you a smile, a hug, or an encouraging word—just enough to change everything.

That's how the undertow works. It holds more than just death; it holds hope and a God who reaches out to bring you through. He strengthens you through this undertow, showing you that you can make it.

No matter how strong the current, how deep the numbness, we must never quit. This world needs you and the purpose you bring to humanity. Fight with everything you have—fight for your loved ones, for life, and against the undertow that seeks to destroy you. Let hope rise to the surface and bring light to a new season! Breathe!

MONSTER
OF
GIFTS &

Behind The Eyes

Some ideas are expressed more clearly in written form than they are orally. But some words are better left unsaid and unwritten.

There are times when thoughts should be left deep in the silence of our minds rather than spoken out loud. We've all experienced moments when, as soon as the words left our mouths, we wished we could take them back.

Then there are times when the ideas in our minds remain unspoken, and they could have saved a life, made a difference, repaired a relationship, or mended a heart. This is the tragedy of silence. When should we speak in a crowded world of words? When should we surrender to the spoken word?

Sometimes I feel like I am the only person on earth who has a consistent conversation with my subconscious and who battles with unspoken words. I wake up at three a.m. and listen to the words deep in my soul, having a complete conversation back and forth. I know you may think that I'm crazy, and to some degree, I will not argue that point.

I have surrendered to knowing my true self, and if that means having an internal dialogue that is not intended for anyone but me, then so be it. All of my stories are written in the silence of my mind before any typing begins. Even as I write now, I am deciding what to write down and what to leave out. It's an active conversation going on between me and my hands.

The words that are deep in my mind may never make it to the pages and to the ears that may or may not need to hear or read those words. It's the life I live, and I am happy in it.

This story may sound like it's about my abusers, but it's not. The truth is simple: It's not you, it's me. These are my words alone, not yours. I don't replay your glances, your tone, your abuse, your cruelty, or even your words. If you were alive, I'm not sure if I would share the thoughts that reside so deeply within my soul.

The darkness, pain, suffering, and unrelenting battle within my soul are something I long to escape. No, you will never hear the words. Even now, long after you are gone, the effects of your words, your torture, and your evil presence remain visible in me. I will never repeat the words you spoke to me; I will never speak of the pain you have caused me.

I will write them as they are life to me; they break the strongholds that have bound me for many years. These words, while simple in nature, are powerful, never said but written. These words are life!

The existential words that I hear may only be for me. The conversations give purpose, reason, and direction. Even now, the struggle to write the exact words is a battle. As you have already seen in this story alone, some words made it to the page that may not have ever made it out of the darkness of my mind. They were shouting to get out, so I let them out. It's my choice in the end. There are more, and maybe one day I will be able to express them.

This story was born from the deep, unspoken conversations in my mind. When those thoughts are finally spoken in confidence or typed out, they become a part of my healing journey. At my age, I continually ask myself what needs to be healed and why I even need to type these stories out. Yet I know that each word and each back-and-forth conversation in my mind brings another day of living, another day of peace, and another day of loving. There was a time when I didn't understand how to love myself or accept love from others. This is an ongoing struggle for me. Some will get this and some will not, and that's okay. Each sentence adds minutes to my life; every story adds months to my life; and every book brings years to me.

My writing is not about me and my journey. I want others to see these conversations and know it's okay to have your own contemplations in your mind. You will make it. Don't quit.

I've left this story alone for weeks now, buried deep in my soul, not sure of the direction or even the message that was evolving. Along the way, I've lost so many friends to these silent battles when they became consumed by the lies they told themselves, so I want to be cautious as I bring this to a close.

The unwritten and unspoken conversations behind closed eyelids have to happen; it's okay. Give yourself grace to speak freely and the strength to voice the unspoken and feel the unwanted. It's difficult, but it's a beautiful way to reconnect with your inner self and nurture your mental and emotional well-being. This grace you give yourself leads to healing and enriches your life in so many ways. These words, spoken or unspoken, will bring you peace and add years to your life. I would be remiss if I didn't advise you: seek professional help if you need it. It's okay.

You all know I am extremely transparent about my therapy. Not that long ago, the voices became so loud and destructive that I didn't think I would make it. I was so close that looking back now it still makes me tremble and shakes me to my core. That's why I'm being vulnerable right now so that you might take a different course. Don't quit! This world needs you, and your purpose is real. You can make a difference with your words, spoken or unspoken. A smile, a hug, a glance, or a comment can change the course of someone's life.

You never know what the conversation is or will be until you speak from behind your eyes. Spoken or not spoken. It's silence that brings the end.

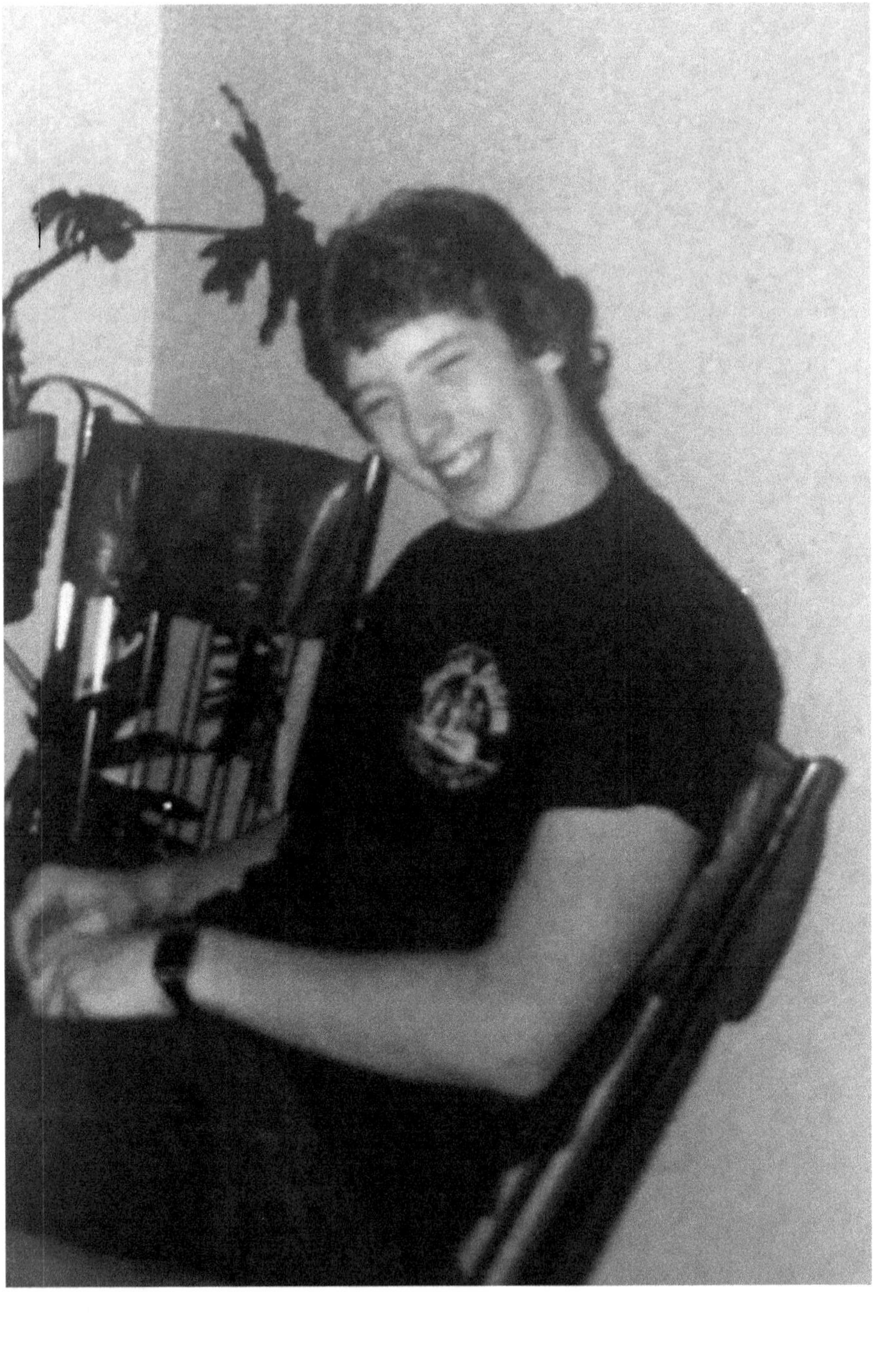

I Saw You

Hey Chris, I saw you today. You were sitting on the rail of the pier, fishing with your friends. You were talking it up as usual and asking questions about the fish in the Cape Fear River. You were probably asking how deep the water is and what kind of bait you should use. This reminds me of how you used to ask those questions in the old days down by the river.

Your beard still looks the same, all spotty with rough patches around your chin. Your hands still look the same—their strength tells the story of a working man. Your voice is still scruffy and harsh sounding, but so soft in tone.

It's the last day of vacation for Lisa and me in Southport, North Carolina. We have fished on the city pier almost every day for the last nine days. Some days were good and other days not so good. We found ourselves staying in room six again at the Riverside Motel. This seems to be a magical place for encounters. There was a tropical storm that rolled through the first couple of days, most likely impacting the fishing. For the most part, our trip was wonderful. People from all walks of life strolled out on the city pier throughout the day. Some just watched as we fished, and some wanted to talk about it.

Today was like all the other days since we've been here; the fishing was slow, and the crowds were large. I'm not sure that we blended in as locals, but they thought we knew what we were doing. Ironically, we were on our last fishing rigs because we had lost all to the rocks below, and we only had a few pieces of bait left. We were far from locals; we were the only people fishing together. No matter the place, we have always enjoyed this togetherness. We listen to stories in stereo and repeat them later in mono to each other. *Did you hear that? Did you hear this one? Oh, wait a minute, did you hear her and the story she told?* These brought smiles and laughter to our souls.

But there was one thing about today that was different. We noticed a tent near the pier and lots of children and parents setting something up. We just thought it was a different vendor, as they frequently came to that area to sell stuff. It was hot on the pier, and there were numerous locals fishing. You can tell who they are; they just look like they belong. I didn't pay much attention to them. I looked mostly at the water and listened to surrounding conversations. That's what I enjoy the most, just listening and waiting for the next story to come to life.

I had just emerged from the grip of a story that had me locked down for months—one of those complex, never-ending pieces that refuse to let you rest. *The Lens* haunted me day and night, demanding my attention. After countless revisions, I finally sent it to my editor, who does beautiful work. As I write this story, it's still with her.

When I am free, I tend to listen more intently and watch people more closely. But the freedom is short-lived—another story is always on the verge of unfolding.

I was listening to several stories today on the city pier. Some were as prescribed, which simply means I could tell you the end before they finished. No big deal—just the way I listen and process.

I've been thinking about a person we met earlier in the week who seemed to be carrying a great deal of pain in her life. I didn't press for any details. As I handed her my book, she simply said, "How did you know I needed this right now?" I wondered if this would be my next story. But it became clear it wasn't—maybe later though.

As we fished, I noticed a group of people coming down the city pier with their children, asking if we would like some lemonade. My knee-jerk response was, "No," without even thinking or looking at who was offering me this sweet, refreshing drink. Then I glanced down. It was a little guy, maybe five or six years old, reaching up towards me with a cup of lemonade, and in his other hand, he held a *pocket Jesus*.

"For you," he said. I melted.

I was... I'm now crying just trying to write this. I was so humbled. So blessed. Moved beyond words. Not worthy of it. Humbled again. Hands in the air—overwhelmed by this unexpected expression of love right there on the city pier.

I took the lemonade and the *little Jesus* and told the boy I had always wanted one of those. I placed it front and center in my tackle box. He also gave me a flower and a card with the name of their church. I was so moved by this that fishing didn't even matter anymore. It was just about that moment and what was happening right then and there.

They continued up and down the city pier, blessing everyone they met.

I was staring at the water below, and this little girl came over to a group of people behind me on the pier who were fishing. She offered the group some lemonade, and they said, "Sure." I held my cup up to toast the girl in the group, and one of them called out in a loud voice, "I know, right?" We acknowledged each other without any other social exchange, but it was great.

I had not paid much attention to this small group of five or six behind me. They were all talking, and they even had some music playing very low. They looked like they were in their thirties or so. The group seemed to be more about just being there than fishing. I thought that was cool.

The parents and children were making another pass to see if anyone needed a new cup of lemonade—or even a little Jesus. As they approached the group behind me, they asked, "Anyone need a lemonade or a Jesus?" One guy said in a very scruffy and harsh voice with a very soft tone to the little guy, "I don't want any lemonade, but I will take a Jesus."

I turned—almost in slow motion—to see who had said this. My eyes followed from the floor of the pier up to the young man sitting on the rail. It was my brother, Chris!

"I'll take Jesus," he said. I stared at this young man, and for a moment, our eyes met. It was as if he was saying, "I'm okay." No words were spoken—just a quiet reassurance he was at peace. That while he was no longer here, he was doing just fine with his Jesus.

Chris passed years ago after a long battle with drugs—a battle he could never win. The pain was too deep. At thirty-seven, his life ended, and his struggle finally gave way to peace. He is the one who introduced me and my family to Jesus. For that, I will always be grateful, and I am happy that he encountered Jesus when he did.

I watched as the young man on the rail hopped down, tucked the little Jesus in his pocket, and walked away. As our eyes met once more, he gave me a glance that seemed to say, "I'm going to be just fine. I have Jesus with me now." I stood there quietly and watched as they disappeared into the crowd.

When my brother left this world, all he had was a few papers in his pocket and a small New Testament Bible. I still have it to this day. This encounter reminded me that all we have in this world is hope. Hope that things are going to be okay. Hope that we are going to make it.

Just like the old days at the river,—we fished, we hoped, and we loved.

It was great to see you today, my brother!

We all need a little Jesus in our lives.

Tapestry

The wind has blown in my direction for many years now, from the east, west, north, and south. Many currents have taken me from there to here. The wind has finally calmed. Where am I? The tapestry is almost finished. The end is near; others say no, but I know it's close.

So many want to be heard, and there is an abundance of talking and influencing happening in our world today. I believe it's an attempt to complete the tapestry. Be it personal or otherwise, the tapestry is woven by what it hears, feels, and experiences.

I've been thinking about this story for months now; it seems more complex than just a woven piece. It's a story that is frayed yet still has a sense of completion. Sadly, every story has an ending, and that's the beauty of the tapestry: it tells the whole story. What will mine look like? What will yours look like? Will they be completed or still marked by frayed ends—threads never told or never healed?

Often called "the rich tapestry of life," this metaphor describes how life is made up of many intertwined parts—threads of experience, memory, and emotion woven together.

The tapestry is unique to each individual—there are no two people who look the same. The colors, the sunrises, the sunsets, the words, the glances, the smiles, the laughter, the conversations, the hugs, the kisses, and the stories that are told are different for everyone.

Our tapestry tells a story. When completed, they hang on a wall of memories that last for a few years and maybe even into the next generation. At the end of our lives, what does it all mean? Is it really a life that says, "I have lived," or a life that says, "I have been broken?" The words I write are for those who are to come and for those who see my tapestry and view it as a complete work or a frayed part of humanity.

The tapestry is meant to make a difference; the colors and the weave of brokenness are all mentioned to bring about change in humanity. The brokenness is meant to bring light to those who need change and hope for a future. When people look at our completed and frayed tapestry, they will see that our struggle was real and that we left a path which was meant to be finished. It forges a path to completeness for those who will follow.

The broken are those who are left behind and never raised to life. The broken are those who never realize that their tapestry matters. The broken are those who never ever know that their tapestry is being written and will be hung on a wall one day in front of all who know their story. Every story will be told one day, and every story matters, and that's the importance of the tapestry.

Woven together, piece by piece and thread by thread, our tapestry is being wondrously constructed. While in the moment, we don't even realize that our tapestry may be nearing its end. Then, suddenly, the weaving slows, our nail is placed on the wall, and we see our tapestry as a whole. What have we left? What have we given? What message have we offered to humanity? Have we completed our mission? Is our tapestry frayed, or is it complete? So many questions arise in this woven pattern of life.

In my own life, I can testify that my tapestry may never be completed, but as best I can, I will strive to weave every frayed thread. My goal is singular: to be at peace in the end, and to weave a tapestry that says *I cared*, that says *I loved*, and that *makes an impact on humanity*. In the end, I want my tapestry to say I was not lonely, that I was alive, blessed by all who knew me, a strength to those whom I encountered, and an encourager to the fallen. My tapestry will speak for itself. Its colors will be vibrant and full, telling a story of completeness and wholeness to all who knew me. The tapestry will tell our story. What will yours look like?

Mine may tell the inspiring story at the ball field last weekend with my grandsons. As a few of my frayed ends were being woven back together that day, I realized some were still healing and some had already been made whole. It felt like the solidarity between me and the tapestry itself. As tears rose to the edges of my eyes, no one knew, and no one saw, as this quiet, sacred moment unfolded.

I was asking a simple question to my nine-year-old grandson. "So why are baseball gloves so expensive, and what's with these baseball bats?" He began to explain in detail the reason for the soft, woven leather, the intricacy of the bat, and why the grip had to have a special wrap. The gloves were woven in fine leather, and the pocket was meant to catch the really fast balls. The pocket was supposed to protect the fingers, which fit into a specific place that helps shield the hands. I was so taken by the conversation. He even demonstrated how to hold his bat and how to swing it. Then he looked up at me and said, "That's how we do it, G Daddy. It's baseball."

I thought about this for a few hours, and after talking to my sweet Lisa, I realized how profoundly this moment had impacted me. I felt as if some of the frayed ends of my tapestry had been woven back into place.

There was so much I had missed as a child. I realized my grandson was experiencing something I had never had the opportunity to see, much less be a part of. I was witnessing a chain, once broken by my own trauma, being mended with love, compassion, and a hope that is real.

At his age, I had been fighting for my life, hiding from the evil that tried to destroy me day and night. I was that invisible child, longing to be seen and fighting to survive. There was no love, no baseball, no basketball, and no fun at all. Just the constant search for a place to rest, even for a moment, which felt like everything at the time.

How blessed I am to be in this moment with my grandson, who has the opportunity simply *to be.* The opportunity to show his G Daddy his tapestry, the exquisite colors being woven in such sweet love. What a beautiful story my daughter and her wonderful husband have written—and continue to write—in his life.

While my own tapestry remains frayed in so many places, I believe these moments in life take those worn pieces of our tapestry and weave them back into place. They complete us. They make us whole. And if we are willing, they bring a special healing to us all.

It's never too late. The tapestry is waiting for you.

Those Golden Shoes

Ecclesiastes 3:14-15 (MSG)
14 I've also concluded that whatever God does, that's the way
it's going to be, always. No addition, no subtraction. God's
done it and that's it. That's so we'll quit asking questions and
simply worship in holy fear.
15 Whatever was, is. Whatever will be, is. That's how it always
is with God.

I was sharing these verses with a friend the other day and realized how impactful they were. It's not our time, but it's God's time. This story is an illustration of how we shouldn't think more highly of ourselves than we ought to because of our status or worldly possessions.

Back in the day, we all played flag football every Thursday. Rick and I were best friends in high school and still are to this day. He had one seat at the very back of the school bus and I had the other. We orchestrated things on the bus from this vantage point. We were not bullies but knew the status and responsibility we had as being the older boys in the home. If we saw something that was out of line, we were quick to act and bring correction.

Looking back, I wonder what the other boys must have thought about how we behaved on those Thursdays.

On Thursdays, Rick and I didn't talk; we just rode home from school on the bus. We played flag football on separate teams. He played on the "farm" team, and I played on the home team. The farm team always recruited the tougher and stronger guys. They were called the farm team because they worked on the farm. By the way, farm work paid seven dollars a week and was one of the highest paying jobs around. The farm team was the best, but I wasn't on it. Don't get me wrong, I was as good as any of those guys, but the farm thing just wasn't me.

When we rode home on Thursdays, the bus was always quiet. This was the day that Rick and I would taunt each other and tell each other exactly what was going to happen on the field that day. You get the point. We were very specific in our language and our action. The other boys would just listen in. If you are wondering who was driving our school bus, it was another boy from the home. We had our own bus, and it was just us.

Then, one day, Rick crosses the line. We are going back and forth; it is a very heated conversation that day and we are almost in a fight, screaming back and forth. Suddenly, Rick stands up and picks up his book bag. The bus driver slams on breaks. As the bus is coming to a stop, I stand up, gripping the back of the seat in front of me. Rick reaches into his book bag and pulls out a pair of freshly painted football cleats. He screams, "Yeah baby. What's up? What are you going to do with these bad boys?" He had painted his football cleats gold. Then he declares at the top of his lungs, "Today, these babies are going to fly by you so fast; you ain't going to see nothing but gold." Then he starts this taunt of "FTD, FTD baby, FTD, FTD baby." When we were growing up, there was a flower guy on a TV commercial that wore golden shoes, and he ran really fast from delivery to delivery. Rick decides that if he wears golden shoes, he will be as fast as the FTD guy.

The whole bus bursts out laughing, the driver starts the bus, and we continue home. Rick straps on his golden shoes, still taunting me. He is dead serious about these shoes. What can I say? The man has golden shoes on. I was so ready to get to the field that day. The game starts, and it doesn't take long for me and Rick to get matched up. He catches a pass and runs down the sideline; he looks at me and points down at his shoes. I head straight for him. When I get within range, I dive and hit him right in the side and send him sailing about twenty feet out of bounds. This is supposed to be flag football, so while we are on the ground, I grab his flag and say, "Got ya, golden boy." We both get up and realize how stupid we have been and laugh out loud. To this day, we still crack up about the *golden shoes*.

So, what's the point of this story? Sometimes our possessions make us think we are something we are not. Things don't really make us who we are. They paint a picture to others, but when it's all said and done and the lights go out, who are you?

As the word in Ecclesiastes says, "Whatever was, is. Whatever will be, is." Put in my vernacular, "It is what it is." If we would try harder at living a life of truth and not one of golden shoes, we could help each other more. Maybe we could team up and do something for this world, leaving our golden shoes in the closet. Be who God made you to be. Find your destiny and your position in life in Jesus Christ. This life is not about how much stuff we can accumulate and how we model the clothes on our backs and the cars in our driveways. Life is about purpose and destiny. Who are you? Where are you going and how are you going to get there? Are you going to be you or someone with golden shoes? Are you going to be authentic or be a painted-on person?

Where My Brother Once Stood

2 Samuel 18:30 (ESV): "And the king said, 'Turn aside and stand here.' So he turned aside and stood still."

I write this story in memory of my brother, Chris, who died at the young age of thirty-seven. It's been almost three years since he passed away. He ran as far as he could and as long as he could. His pain and suffering never left him. Finally, it took his life.

This picture is where he once stood. Chris and I had many memories on this pier, sitting there in the night hours with a dim light in the background, just enough to light up our faces. The sounds of the water were so calm, and to this day, I still hear the silence. The conversations were always light and never too deep. Home would come up now and then, but we mostly talked about the future. Chris talked about his hopes and dreams, and I talked about mine.

Today, I visited the pier again, thinking of him and recalling the beautiful memories we had there. I usually stand right where he stood, look out over the water, and listen as if to hear his voice, but there is nothing but silence now. This is truly a special place and not just because this is where my brother once stood. This is also where my girls have stood, where many of my friends have stood, and where the love of my life now stands, my sweet Lisa. I love you, Lisa!

As Lisa and I sat there today, I carved our initials into the wood once again. I often do this because I forget where I have carved our initials in the past. There are hundreds of names carved on this pier. This tells me of all the others that have once stood here. Not just Boys Home boys and girls, but many in the community and many who came to vacation at Lake Waccamaw. Many dreams of love and a future were born here; the carvings tell me so.

I was reminded today by an old and new friend of just how short life can be. I called my friend for the first time in some thirty years. Her voice sounded the same as it did thirty years ago as she said, "We can't meet today; someone has died, and we will be going to the funeral home." As I listened to her explain, I was sad, not to miss our meeting, but for all of those who once had hopes and dreams like Chris. I was sad for those who loved her, and I knew what pain and suffering they were going through. As I walked out to the end of that pier today and stood where my brother once stood, I was reminded that life is brief, and it seems to take us places we never thought we would go. My journey has been filled with adventures, great joy, and many heartaches; I know am blessed to still be standing where my brother once stood.

There are so many twists and turns on this journey of life. Many people try to explain the twists and turns, but they cannot. For me, it is where my brother once stood. The memories I have will be part of me until I no longer stand. Then others will walk the same path as I have and stand where I stood and say, "I once stood here." The water will whisper the hopes and dreams they had and will tell stories of the many who have stood there.

We serve a wonderful God who has allowed me into so many lives, both the standing and the once stood. I am thankful to each of you for sharing your lives with me, not just your hopes and dreams, but what has crushed you and caused you pain and suffering, what has turned your dreams into nightmares, and what has cursed you for a lifetime.

To end this story is impossible, as life continues. To apply this story to your life and mine, we must stand where our brothers and sisters once stood. Leaning on their memories, their hopes, and their dreams. Remembering all the good of life and how blessed we are to still be where they once stood. I love you, Chris; thank you for the memories, the hopes, and the dreams of where you once stood.

Never let go of your hopes and dreams. This is where you stand today!

Pride & Priority

What do you know to be true in your life? What drives you to make decisions in life? Is it pride or is it priority?

We all talk about the priorities of our life and how they drive our schedules and dictate our timetables. They tell us when to sit and when to stand, when to go and when to come. One could say that priorities are the driving force in every decision we make. I think this is an accurate statement, but there is a greater force behind each decision we make, and it's called *pride*. In some ways, pride enters every decision we make, and whether we like it or not, pride wins more times than we care to admit.

We are all so busy and there seems to be no time left for God. There is no time left for the things in life that really make a difference. There is no time to say, *I love you*, no time to give a hug, no time to lend a helping hand, and no time to ask a friend if they need to talk about something.

Do we really have that much going on in our lives? If we say God is in control, then why do we have so much to do? Why is our schedule so jam-packed with *to do* things? One answer may be pride!

I met a lady a few years ago who had seven adopted children, all with special needs. I asked myself, *how does she do that*? How does she take care of all those children plus come to the lake for a day of fun? I believe she was just proud to be a mom. Her pride was in her children and in doing what, as she said, "God called her to do." Lisa and I had all we could handle with two healthy girls. I believe this lady's pride was in the right place. That's just me looking from the outside in. Things are not always what they seem when it comes to pride.

Pride is masked easily; it can be covered quickly with a word, and it can be made invisible to everyone on the outside by counter actions of *fill-ins*. That's when we feel guilty about our behavior, and instead of calling it pride, we mask it by *filling* our schedule with good works to justify our former actions. You are the only one who truly knows the truth and the motive behind every choice you make. Is it a priority or is it pride that makes you decide what choice to make?

We do a great deal of things in the name of Jesus just because of pride. When God is using us mightily, the test is always there to see where our pride lies. The moment we step in front of God and elevate ourselves above Him, we find ourselves back where we started and must start all over again. That is pride. You should be proud of the place you hold in the kingdom and the way God has brought you through trials, but be careful in bringing the priority of pride with you.

What role does priority play when it comes to pride? You tell me! Is it a priority that your place in the community is noticed? Is it a priority that you hide who you really are from others? Is it a priority that people only see the *Jesus* side of you? We spend a great deal of time and energy building ourselves up to who we think we are and who God expects us to be.

How do you place pride in your life? What priority do you give it? It is your decision. You are the only one in control of your pride. To sum this up, it's a battle. We all battle priority and pride. The goal is to have pride and priority live together in harmony. While pride is always seeking to elevate self and dictate the priority we place in any circumstance, our goal should be to seek the kingdom of God first.

Pride grows from a lack of setting God's priorities in our lives. When you want something, pride steps in and has an influence on your decision. An example of that is when you worry about what others will think. If you are overly concerned with the opinion of others, then pride is standing at the door and already has an influence on your decision. Am I saying we should never care what others think? Not at all. Kingdom thinking requires us to ask what God thinks first.

Remember that pride is controlling and seeks self-centered attention, while priority requires you to weigh the significance of an action to find its rightful place in the mix of life's schedule.

The outlook for priority is to seek first the kingdom of God. When we put God first, pride will play a smaller role in our lives.

The Ellie Inn

We have all heard the expression: *if these walls could talk, what would they say*? Use your imagination and join me on this explorative journey. Stop for one moment. Stop scrolling. Stop looking at the reels. Give social media a break and listen to the walls speak. Listen to the echoes of times past. Hear the people whisper; hear the forever of history cry out.

Have you ever walked into a place and thought about the history, the memories, the pain, the joy, and the life-changing words that may have been spoken there? I'm sure all of you have walked into a room and been met by a memory—the scent of it, the glance it brings, the smile it evokes, and even the hug that it offers.

I recently had an encounter at The Ellie Inn, which is adjacent to my neighborhood. As I entered the front door of this magnificent place, I could hear the memories of humanity as well as the dreams and hopes of its visitors. I heard laughter and, of course, sadness. This was our first visit to this magical place.

Let me give you a bit of the history of this exquisite place, as the owners describe it. *Nestled in Fuquay-Varina, North Carolina, The Ellie Inn is a restored 1900s schoolhouse, perfect for intimate gatherings and special events.*

The Ellie Inn is more than just a place to stay; it's an experience where history and elegance come together. Every room retains unique details from its schoolhouse past while offering the modern amenities and conveniences needed for a comfortable stay. The charm of Ellie Nicholson's legacy and the inviting atmosphere of this beautifully preserved home provide guests with a sense of timeless warmth and comfort.

Whether you're celebrating life's special moments, seeking a unique gathering place, or simply wanting a peaceful getaway, The Ellie Inn promises a one-of-a-kind experience. Here, the echoes of history enrich your memories, creating a backdrop for celebration, relaxation, and connection.

Right from the owner's description, I heard the echoes and voices of those who have been in these rooms. How wonderful is this journey, and how marvelous is this place that speaks so loudly from history. This is where this story was born: from the place of *if these walls could talk*.

I have scheduled a time this week to sit and listen to the walls at The Ellie Inn. The owners were so gracious to allow me to write about this unique encounter.

The Ellie Inn is a writer's haven; it has all the components a writer needs. How blessed I am to have this experience. I feel like there may have been other writers before me in this place; I will find out soon because I will listen as the walls talk. They will tell me.

I've arrived at the inn. I have this excited and anxious feeling in my soul. It's hard to explain. I'm hoping that this will subside as I start to write. It's not in the way at all, but the uncertainty of this story may be the cause. I'm exploring new territory emotionally. This place is magnificent!

I first settled into a cozy spot near the stairway, a little area I've come to think of as the parlor, and later moved into the main entertaining space to continue writing. I am now sitting in a chair that wraps around me with a pillow under my left arm. As I look up at these walls, I wonder what has been said in this room. The dreams that were shared here, the lessons learned here, the names spoken here, and the visions that were discussed here. These walls are some twenty feet tall, and a sophisticated brown, textured ceiling crowns them. Their beauty sings new songs now. The past is gone, but the stories that speak here remain.

I've finally calmed into a state where my mind and fingers move together, with no thoughts getting in the way. It feels like a river, carrying the stories of The Ellie Inn. My mind keeps telling my fingers to slow down. The river doesn't need to rush. These stories are numerous, and this is not the end of the project. Take your time, my friend. Enjoy the writing. This is a special story.

There is exuberant laughter here; the echoes are so audible and melodic, and it's emotional for me as I hear them. My experiences as a child and later as a young person consisted of more survival than happiness. These feelings come unexpectedly in this place. I see myself in the corner of the room, curled up on the floor, in a time when hope was gone, and only sadness and the shadow of death filled my soul.

The corner is my safe place right now as I listen to these stories.

The joy is flowing all around me; it's a river of laughter swirling around the room, like a whirlpool of grace, mercy, peace, and harmony. It's a virtual vortex of love. As I sit in the corner in my own alternate world, thinking no one sees me, arms start to reach out to me from this whirlpool of love. They start to sing in unison: "Holy, holy, holy, bring your pain to the throne of grace and mercy." The room is spinning faster and faster, and there are more and more now reaching out to me. As I lift my head, I can see others in the corners of the room. We make eye contact, and our hands start to move away from our curled position.

This vortex of grace and mercy is swirling at a life-giving pace now, and I can see the faces of these radiant angels reaching out to me. I can see what's written on their dreams and their hopes. It's so extraordinary. I want to reach out, but I'm just not sure if I can. I've been here so long. *Will I be here forever?* I ask myself. *Will I take a step and reach out to humanity and trust again?* I glance around the room and view the corner across from me. I witness him reaching out his arms, and see the whirlpool gently pulling him in as if they have rescued a soul from the depths of darkness. At this moment, rejoicing erupts in this vortex of love, mercy, and grace. I hear the angels cry in an overwhelming sound of love. Will I be next? I'm so resistant at this moment.

I want to move to a different space in the inn, but I can't right now. The others must be rescued in all corners of the room. As one leaves, another takes his place. This is where hope lives. I have to stay for now. I know there are other spaces in the inn that need this sea of love to rescue them. But here I am in this space, still in the corner, but more alert now, slightly reaching out with my fingertips. I am more interested in seeing others rescued than taking care of my own rescue.

I remember names from my past who were rescued by this whirlpool of love, mercy, and grace: Chris (my brother), Kevin (my best friend), Tammy (an important part of my story), Lisa (my wife), my sister, my mom, Keith (my friend), my dad, Matt (the son of Kevin and Tammy), and Shirley (a beautiful friend). So many in this glorious sea of love have peace now. I'm reaching out just a bit more now, experiencing the peace that is spoken in this place; I'm not sure if I am ready just yet.

As the whirlpool slows, I can clearly see the arms of those who are still reaching out to me, inviting me to the table of healing, the table of love, and the table that represents the beauty of humanity. They are singing, "Come now, get up and start this journey. It won't be easy but it's a start. Let the pain stay in the corner, let the suffering die, and let the deserving be where they belong. This is not your fault." The voices are loud as we face this reality of decisions. Will you come? Will you reach out and be one who comes to this place and now helps those who will come behind you? There are so many. It's up to you to reach out. Your name needs to be written here. Lift your hands and join us.

All we have to do is come to the inn and sit, listen, and be ready for the rescue. Love, joy, peace, and harmony; it's a new beginning for us all.

I must admit this whirlpool of mercy and grace is breathtaking. Its white, flowing clouds spin so slowly that I can see the vapors disappear at my fingertips as I touch them. I'm in the midst of a magnificent pool of gold, rubies, and turquoise colors, and nothing is hindering me from joining this place. And yet I'm always drawn by them—the others that need this more than me.

I'm still not sure if it's my time. I'm still working on myself, and I am hopeful that one day I will reach the place where I can completely heal. For now, I am standing in the corner and content with watching those who are pulled into the whirlpool of love, mercy, and grace. It's okay to be you and to acknowledge that healing is happening. As long as you are here, you will have hope. Don't quit now; renewal is happening here.

The Ellie Inn is waiting, and these lovely walls will always exude love, grace, and mercy. There will always be a whirlpool of hope here. Come experience this magnificent place of history. Will you join us here?

Burying the Foxes

This story is one that has many memories tied to it. It was written two months after I joined the ministry, May 2005. Many excuses have risen since that time, many foxes buried. John and I skied the other day and it reminded me of this story. As with all of the stories I've written, I feel a need to edit them some. This one was in need of a verse. I have been going through some things lately and as always going to the word seems to direct me just the right way. This week I was challenged on "why are you not ________? I had no excuse, only to realize that God led me to these verses in Ephesians this morning and this has helped me answer the question I was asked. They match this story perfectly and more than that they match my life right now.

> Ephesians
> 1-3 In light of all this, here's what I want you to do. While I'm locked up here, a prisoner for the Master, I want you to get out there and walk—better yet, run!—on the road God called you to travel. I don't want any of you sitting around on your hands. I don't want anyone strolling off, down some path that goes nowhere. And mark that you do this with humility and discipline—not in fits and starts, but steadily, pouring

> yourselves out for each other in acts of love, alert at noticing differences and quick at mending fences.
> 4-6 You were all called to travel on the same road and in the same direction, so stay together, both outwardly and inwardly. You have one Master, one faith, one baptism, one God and Father of all, who rules over all, works through all, and is present in all. Everything you are and think and do is permeated with Oneness.
> 7-13 But that doesn't mean you should all look and speak and act the same. Out of the generosity of Christ, each of us is given his own gift.

This will be the first weekly update I have ever titled. You will find out towards the end why it's titled. Keep in mind these are not scripted and never looked for but are from my heart and reflections of what God has done in my life this week or brought to memory something that needed to be put into words as this is a continual healing process for me.

This is my fourth season skiing. I am a late starter but been around water most of my life. I have been a believer since 1988. Lisa and I were saved during a Wednesday night service, how unusual is that. I should have known then God had something very unusual in mind for us in our service for Him. To be quite honest my skiing has lead me on this journey. It seems God has given me something each week to tie skiing in with our Christian walk since accepting His call to IHW. I have tried to not write but it just has got to be.

This week has been no different. The title is a tribute to the person that this analogy came from. His name is John. He is the very one that God put me in touch with when we first started to ski on a course.

I want you to think about something, all you water skiers! What is the one thing we all talk about or tell stories about, either while warming up or I sometimes wait until we get on the back of the boat to talk about. Their I am putting on my ski, talking as usual and out "they" come. What are "they". Have you traced the steps or your routine. I want you to really think about this before I tell you. What do we do before we get in the water, sometimes we wait until after the first pass, drop at the other end, and out "they" come. Sometimes like last week we wait until we make some of the ugliest runs and have some of the very worst skiing in history. We climb back in the boat shaking our head and here "they" come. Have you figured out what I am talking about yet? It's those excuses. John shared with me the mother of all excuses. It is without doubt the best I had ever heard. You will not guess what the man said!

He falls into telling me about this dead fox near his house. I don't think he really knew what to do with it. He said he grab the shovel and started digging the hole to bury the fox, he said he even dug little holes for the legs. I can see this hole and more than that I can see the old dead fox standing in the hole, upright and covered up. I think this is how the story went. The point being his skiing may not be good today because he had to bury the fox. He had to dig the hole. I have heard many excuses, the wind, rain, snow, boat wake, not my handle, ran 10 miles this morning, rode 25 miles to get over here on my bike, broke my ribs. You all have a list and know what I am talking about.

Do you see the relation here with our Christian walk. When God gives us a task to do, to serve Him in some other way than perfect conditions we start to make excuses, at least I do. Don't feel bad, Moses did to, "who am I Lord" he said. This weekend it was the wind for me, before I left the dock, I had the excuse ready. If I don't ski well today it's because of the wind! Guess what, with that attitude I didn't ski well. I had to fight for everything

I got today. Was it the wind. NO!! It was my attitude towards the course that was set before me. When God puts the course in front of us we always seem to rush to make excuses why we can't do it that way. Excuses are very powerful. Sometimes they are helpful because they lead us to where God wants us, they help direct our path and are part of our decision process, we can learn from our excuses. Notice this is not the same as a mistake, we make excuses in order not to make the so called mistakes.

The conditions are not always going to be perfect. I am so convinced this is why God can only show us small parts of His course for our life. We would start making excuses of why we could not do it that way. Not only was this real for me this week but I had a tough question to ask and to answer. It was one of those questions that we try to stay away from because we really don't' know the answer and try to say "does it really matter". But somebody gave real good advice "George, you need to find this answer for yourself, don't ask man, don't rely on what you were taught, seek God out and ask, go to the word. I had made every excuse not to, "didn't matter, we can just do things a different way. Something just drove me on and kept saying "what ever you do, "no excuses and no compromises. What ever the out come!

God blessed me this week by giving me an answer to my question. It really does not matter what the question was. The point is how I got to the answer. How many excuses did God have to go through with me to get to the answer. You guys have been skiing way longer than me so I know your excuse bank is rich. How about our Christian walk, how rich is our spiritual excuse bank? How often does God want to do something and we just make a quick withdraw! No, can't do that, because ______? You fill in the blank. Let's go this week and try hard to do what God has ask us to do without excuse.

Don't feel bad when we make an excuse or bury a fox, we are just human you know, it is our nature and will always be a part of our thought process. We love to bury foxes. Does this mean we have to say yes to every little thing someone ask us. NO! It all goes back to what we all have talked about in the past months. Ask GOD! Ask about the big things and the little things. A reason is different from an excuse, it is a different thought process. This week I want to encourage us all to not make too many withdraws and to ease up on the deposits in our excuse banks.

Nowhere To Run

Isaiah 49:8 (MSG) God also says: "When the time's ripe, I answer you. When victory's due, I help you. I form you and use you to reconnect the people with me, To put the land in order, to resettle families on the ruined properties."

Have you ever wondered why we do things that don't make a great deal of sense? Is it God's will or our will? This is an age-old question that is not answered by just a brief comment or letter. In studying this week and through conversations, I have decided that it's okay to sit still for a minute or two. It's okay to let God redirect you onto a fresh path. It's hard not to run ahead of God and start something new and exciting. I see many pieces of a great puzzle, but none fit together yet. For the past few months, I have been running back and forth in my mind. I am tired of running, so I am walking and listening now.

I remember a guy I grew up with at one of the homes I lived in. His name was Philip Myers. If you ever went anywhere with him, you had better be in shape. He always wanted to run. He came over to our cottage one day and asked if we could make a trade. I said, "Sure, that sounds like a great deal." The only problem was, the stuff he was trading for was across campus. So off we went.

The second we stepped out the door, he took off. I was a runner back in the day, so it was no problem keeping up with him. In the midst of our sprint to the other side of the campus, I asked him why he ran everywhere he went. He replied quickly, "You never get anywhere in life by walking; it takes too much time. I have pondered this statement for many years, and I have often wondered if he is still running or if he finally slowed down and enjoyed the beauty around him.

His philosophy on running can be taken many ways. We can run everywhere we go, and that can be good, but you may get tired or run right past the very thing God has for you.

To live a life of victory, we need to know where to run. Once God has given you a task, take off like we did. Remember, we made the deal in the cottage, and we knew where to run. We had direction.

The deals we make with God will be on our knees. Then we need to step out, take off, and run with purpose. God can keep up.

The Accident

It was a beautiful evening in October, one of those Friday nights I will never forget. I had the task of taking the guys to the movies on that night. Not sure how I ended up with this duty, being only sixteen years old at the boy's home, but it gave me an opportunity to show some responsibility. Sometimes we drove station wagons, but that night I was driving the big van, a fifteen-passenger Dodge van.

Whiteville was eleven miles from the lake, a straight shot on highway 74-76. I had driven this route many times, taking the guys to the movies. On this particular Friday, I didn't care to stay and watch the movie, so I dropped the boys off and came back to the lake. Not sure why I came back but I did.

Around nine-thirty, I was getting ready to go back to Whiteville to pick up the guys. I knew the movie would end soon. On the way out the door, Bobby and Preston asked if they could ride with me. I said, "Sure, let me make a couple of banana sandwiches to carry with me." I used to love those things.

Heading up highway 74-76, I passed the graveyard and the one-hundred-acre pecan grove with Spanish moss hanging in the trees, which was kind of spooky at night. I passed the sandwich shop that was never open, and then I entered the small town of Hallsboro, right past our high school.

I had already eaten both sandwiches before getting to Hallsboro, and this was just four miles into the trip. When I passed the high school, I reached down for my seat belt. I had it in my hand and decided that I wasn't going to wear it. I never did, but I had picked it up and was about to latch it, but then said, "Forget it, I don't need that thing." I had glanced at my speedometer, and I was at the perfect speed of forty-five miles an hour. The police were never really bad in that area. I just remember being at that speed and looking at the fingerprinted glass on the instrument panel.

Approaching the intersection of state road 1001 and highway 74-76, everything was great. Then, out of nowhere, a car appeared in my windshield. Everything went into slow motion, almost like a dream. The van went into a tumble after hitting a car that had run the stop sign.

I was ejected out of the tumbling van through the windshield, and I found myself about one-hundred feet from the wreckage. I stood up and wondered into the highway and was making my way down to the hardware store. My body was covered in blood, and I was shaking violently. My destination seemed so far away. I looked over at the van, which was now across the road, and saw people fighting. I didn't know what had happened to Preston or Bobby. I had my eyes fixed on that hardware store. There I felt the arms of a friend come around me, giving me his coat. He told me everything was going to be okay. I was slipping into shock moment by moment. My body was numb to the pain.

The ambulance had arrived, and they ushered me off to the hospital in Whiteville. There they checked me out, and I gave up my banana sandwiches I had eaten earlier. My body realized the pain I was in. They decided to transfer me to Wilmington because my skull was crushed in one place, and I had internal bleeding.

I would spend the next few weeks in the hospital. My face and body were scarred from the wreck. I found out that Preston had taken several hundred stitches, and Bobby had a broken leg. Bobby was also beaten up at the wreck by the family of the girl who was riding in the car I had hit. They didn't know what had happened or whose fault it was. All they knew was their sister was dead. My soul was now scarred by the news of her death. Her brother was in my graduating class. My return to school was extremely difficult, but my friends made it easier. Many of whom thought I had died that night.

After many years, I still have the scars of this accident; my head is still numb, and my jaw still pops when I talk sometimes. The real scars are much deeper. They are the ones that make me wonder *what if*? I wonder what if I had left a second or two later? What if I had not made those sandwiches? What if I had reached down and put my seat belt on? Even though I didn't know Jesus Christ at that time, I believe in the total sovereignty of God. God knew then and still knows today what will come my way. He is and always has been in control of life. There are no accidents with God! Do you believe in the sovereignty of God? Who is in control? When trouble is in the air, who do you turn to? When the still voice in your heart says, "Buckle up. Trouble is on the way. Be ready," what is your response?

I didn't listen. I threw it back and said, "I don't need this thing." Years have gone by now, and I understand the providential will of God. Now that I know Jesus Christ, I recognize His still voice.

Sometimes I listen and sometimes I don't. He reminds me by saying, "Didn't I tell you to buckle up?" Life isn't an easy road, but it can be a road of wondrous journeys and many blessings. One of the greatest joys of my life is the relationships God has allowed me to have with many of you. God has used you to walk with me in trials and in glory. The *what ifs* in life belong to God. Is there a *what if* in your life? Give it to the sovereign God who created all things.

1 Peter 1:18-21 (MSG)
"Your life is a journey you must travel with a deep consciousness of God. It cost God plenty to get you out of that dead-end, empty-headed life you grew up in. He paid with Christ's sacred blood, you know. He died like an unblemished, sacrificial lamb. And this was no afterthought. Even though it has only lately—at the end of the ages—become public knowledge, God always knew he was going to do this for you. It's because of this sacrificed Messiah, whom God then raised from the dead and glorified, that you trust God, that you know you have a future in God."

Not The Plan

Psalm 31: 8, 24 (NIV)
8 You have not handed me over to the enemy but have set my feet in a spacious place.
24 Be strong and take heart, all you who hope in the LORD.

Most of my fondest memories took place in the summer months. The summers of my teen years were full of fun and what I call *life lessons*. I remember all my summers being extremely hot summers. Maybe it's because I lived near the lake and could go and cool off. It seemed like every summer was different, and to this day, they continue to be that way. No summer has ever been the same and has always had one or two of those life lessons tucked away, waiting for me.

In my later teen years, we all wanted to be our own people; we were developing into what our environments had programmed us to be. We were products of our surroundings. If you think about it, we all are. We do and think like those that are around us. There were few exceptions to this rule.

At our high school, we were known as the *boy's home boys*. You could spot one of us a mile away. We tried hard to blend in, and some of us were successful in doing this. One of my best friends had helped me to make this transition from the *smoking area* group to the *A-B* group. Although I would go between groups, Amy had taken an interest in me. She said it was my *curls*. We never dated or fell in love; we were the best of friends and still are to this day. Amy had some friends who were really pretty. Paula was one of them. Paula had long blonde hair, the prettiest eyes I had ever seen, and was chiseled out of a mold that would melt any teenager's heart.

I was in *love*. Paula and I would meet up at school and sit under this big oak tree at lunch, talking about everything in life. I was so nervous to be around her; she was so beautiful. Amy would join us from time to time; I think she was making sure I was treating her friend just right. Amy would often coach me on the things women want to hear—what to say, what not to say.

Amy had arranged for us to meet on Friday and Saturday nights at her house. Amy's parents were so nice. They were the first and only parents I knew who would allow a *boy's home boy* into their house, let alone around their daughter. We would go over and meet up, sitting in the formal area of the house. First, just talking and then making out. Not the kind of making out of today. This was what I would call *monitored* making out. Amy's parents weren't stupid; they kept a close eye on all of us. They were right on the other side of the wall. If I remember correctly, there were no doors to this formal living room. They had beautiful furniture; Paula and I would take one seat and Amy and her date would take the other. I guess you could call it a *double date* at the house.

Amy's mom was beautiful also; she had a heart that just breathed love. Her eyes could tell you anything. Her dad was always nice and stern in his commands to Amy. This was a model that I would use later in life.

I dated one of the most beautiful girls in school. This gave me something that I had never had before—confidence. A confidence that would soon teach me a lesson about life and love. Paula and I were getting along great, loving every minute of our teenage years. Then it happened. This tall, long-legged blonde girl walked by us one day. I had seen this girl before but never really noticed her until now. Her name was Gina. Was it the confidence I had from dating Paula that made me notice her? Was it the fact that she was at the top of the *A* group, along with her sister? Or was it the fact that I had Paula and couldn't have Gina?

I must admit, I was happy in my relationship with Paula and did not need to date another girl or even look at another girl. Paula was a beauty queen. Gina didn't even know my name, and maybe that was the problem. I got up the nerve to talk to Gina. She was very shy and quiet. She was not a talker and didn't seem to be interested in me, so I backed off and continued my relationship with Paula. But there was a problem. A problem that I had not foreseen.

Amy found out that I wanted to talk with Gina. I will never forget standing under the walkway at the entrance to the school. Amy told me it wasn't right to talk to Gina and say I was in love with Paula. After all, Paula was one of Amy's best friends but so was I. Was she going to turn me in? Would she tell Paula? All I had done was try to talk to the girl, but deep in my heart, I knew if Gina would have said *yes,* I would have ended the relationship with Paula. I think this is what Amy knew, too. She knew me better than anyone.

Then Paula asked Amy if she should break up with me. Amy, without hesitation, told her to end our relationship. There were no hard feelings at all; we remained friends throughout high school, and I lost contact with her after we all graduated.

Amy and I remained best friends. When we get together, it's always fun bringing up these stories that truly had an impact on our lives. Looking back, you can see God working. A few years later, I would meet the woman of my dreams, Lisa, and I have been married for twenty-three years now. We have raised two wonderful daughters and have been blessed with more than enough. God used all these little things in life to make the big things seem easier. It's His plan after all.

I believe you can pick out many life lessons in this story. When we have what we want, we always want more. We always seem to feed on wanting some things that just aren't meant for us.

God has a plan for your life. Sure, this was high school and everyone makes mistakes in high school. Some of my best friends made the most life-changing decisions in high school. Some decided to have sex and have babies; some decided to kill people; and some even decided to take their own life.

This story, as with all the others, doesn't seem to end. It's still ongoing. So, what can I use here to apply to my life? I suppose you can say two things. One, God is in complete control of your life, no matter what you think or where you are at. His plan for you has been set out before the beginning of time. We make poor decisions and do stupid things, but the God who holds the universe on its axis and ushers in billions of stars every night has a plan, and you really can't mess it up.

The second thing is that every experience in life is placed in your path for a purpose. It may not be a mountain, and it may not be a valley, but these experiences mold us into the people we become.

In a final word, there is nothing wrong with wanting more, wanting something different, or wanting something new. But be content with what you have and take nothing that has ever happened to you for granted; there is a reason and a purpose behind everything. God will use it for good, no matter how bad it was or how bad it is

The Catfish Pond

It all started about 1975. I was in a startup group home for boys called the Haven House, located on Shepherd Street right off Hillsborough Street in Raleigh. There was a great deal of controversy surrounding the establishment of this group home in the beautiful neighborhood of the small Raleigh community.

The neighbors were not happy about our arrival. I was number eight out of ten boys who would live there for the next year. There was really no time limit to our stay; that was just their best estimate.

To bring this into perspective, there were ten at-risk boys living in a home situated in a beautiful community near Cameron Village and the Rose Garden. What does this have to do with a catfish pond? It has everything to do with that pond, as that's where it was created.

Let me list the wonderful and inspiring individuals who were house parents at the Haven House. There was Peter. All he did was write all day long, documenting our stories as they were happening. There was Barbra. She wore a long robe and flip-flops and smoked a pipe. I can still smell that pipe till this day. The pleasant aroma of the pipe matched her beauty; she was always asking, "Are you ok? Are you doing well?" Then there was Michael, who was the hippie of the group. He was composed and consistently worked to calm us down and keep the peace, always striving to defuse situations and support us at-risk kids. I'm not sure if this group knew what they signed up for. Nonetheless, Michael was up for the challenge. He would gather us up a few times a week to teach us how to connect with our inner being; he called it meditation. We had a name for it, but you probably don't want to know what it was. We were just teenagers trying to figure out life and how we fit in.

He always sat us in a circle in an upstairs room and told us to close our eyes and imagine a pond, a beautiful sun, grass fields, light wind, and earth on our skin. He told us to breathe in and out, inhale and exhale, until we were at a place of solace. A tranquil place of peace! It actually worked. We sat for hours like this, and when we came out of this state, we seemed to be different people. The peace and this place of safety gave us hope. Despite the pain, suffering, and destruction we faced, we had hope that we would make it one more day. I adopted this way of life at an early age and named this place the *catfish pond*. Each one of us there never saw the place the same, just as it is in life.

The catfish pond is where I would go when trouble was on the horizon or seemed to be near to me. It was a place of solitude that brought me freedom and comfort. It was my safe place. It was where I was taught to go to in my time of need. It calmed me and brought me peace. Then life happened, and I left Haven House and 28 Shepherd Street became a memory. A wonderful memory it was.

Over the next few years, I would often go to the catfish pond, remembering those breathing exercises that brought me to that wonderful place.

Some forty-seven years later, I would find myself in a place full of stress, exhaustion, and lack of life. I found myself sitting in the place I had been familiar with in my younger years, the therapy couch. If you have read my other stories, you know that I am extremely transparent about my therapy.

I'm not suggesting that we should rely solely on therapy, but that we all need support in sorting things out from time to time.

God is wondrous, and He has placed extraordinary people in our lives for a reason. My therapist is not only a professional but also a good friend. I often say our paths have crossed in a remarkable way, and I am grateful for that.

We are almost three years in, and I'm still learning about me and the details that have helped me to become me. So how does the catfish pond fit in this story, you may ask? Well, about a year into my sessions, the therapist decided to ask me to do some breathing exercises. *Oh my*, I thought, *let's do this*. As we breathed in and out, she said, "Relax, deep breaths, inhale, exhale, deep breaths. In through your nose and hold it, then exhale. Let's do that again and again." The breathing exercise can go on for a minute to several minutes; it just depends on your mental state.

Then it appeared out of nowhere; the catfish pond was right in front of me. I hadn't been there for more than forty-seven years. It was still as beautiful as ever.

I can see it now; it has changed so much, but it's still so magnificent. The glowing sunshine, perfect temperature, blue skies, and lovely green grass flowing in the wind. There are new things here at the catfish pond. A small stream flowing into the pond that reads on the surface: *peace, joy, love, and harmony*.

As I try to enter it, I am met by an outer ring of exquisite white crystal-like sand. As I walk through it, it's not like sand you and I think about, but it looks like diamonds with the same texture as sand. It's about a twelve-foot-wide ring that is met by a dome of sorts.

You can't enter here if you are stressed. I think for a moment during my journey there: *this is where I can come to relieve my stress and seek peace and harmony in my life*. The voice continues to say, "Breathe, inhale, exhale," until I am allowed to enter into the place of peace, harmony, love, and joy. I step into this place and know instantly that I am where I am supposed to be. The catfish pond has grown so much over the past forty-seven years. I walk in and am greeted by many friends and family. Not much talking at all, more observing.

Let me describe what is in this pond. First, it's not just a pond but a glorious and vast body of water. It's turquoise, and the shore has white sand. There are so many people there resting in peace. I know all of them.

I believe this is the place where Jesus speaks because this is His place. The dome above sprinkles down mercy, grace, peace, joy, and love. Just like the stream that follows into this place.

At the catfish pond, my beautiful Lisa is smiling at me and is right by my side, holding my hand. She motions to me that it's going to be okay. My grandchildren are fishing there, but the fish are unlike any you could ever imagine. The catfish are talking to the children and playing along with them while they swim on their fishing pole lines. They are enjoying the peace and solace that this activity brings all of us.

When you step into this place, you are instantly void of all outside influences. Over to the right of the pond, I see my mom relaxing. She smiles at me as to say, "Thank you." I see my brother, Chris, who loved to fish, standing by my grandchildren, teaching them the things an expert fisherman would teach. He's found peace in his life finally. My daughters are here, resting and relaxing with their husbands. The therapist is here, observing the dynamics of this place and how it significantly contributes to bringing peace and harmony to humanity.

Then there is this reality. There are others here as well. I can't see them, but I sense them in my spirit. They are searching for the same peace that I am experiencing here. There are times I can speak a name and they will answer to that. I know they are searching for the same thing I am—peace, love, harmony, and joy. My friends from my past, who have gone by the way of their own demise, are here. I'm not sad they are here; they create no drama here. I wish for them to experience what I have: peace in this world, joy in my soul, and harmony in my spirit. Love encompasses all of this.

There are those who try to invade the catfish pond, but they cannot. For the most part, I am unaware of this but feel their presence from time to time. There are only a few rules to enter into this place: no drama, no hate, and no confusion. The fountain of mercy and grace that flows here is immeasurable. The joy that is rained down here is more than we can take in, and love is abounding in this place. It's amazing grace!

The dome of the catfish pond is vast and contains miles of transparent words that circle it like a covering, speaking of joy, hope, love, and harmony; join us in this. It speaks the name of Jesus, declaring the hope of life and the peace that He brings us. Whatever you make of this place, it has grown over the past forty-seven years and now is a place that I visit often.

His name is power; His name is Jesus; and His name is life. He has broken so many strongholds in my life here, bringing me the healing that I so desperately needed.

Let Him heal you! Do you think you want to visit the catfish pond? Close your eyes and start the journey.

you are
loved

Words

In this story, I think it's necessary to defend and define my addiction. That's not the purpose of the story, but it would help you read it more clearly without wondering who and what I am talking about.

Addiction and obsession carry a heavy stigma. I'm not concerned with what you might think of me—this isn't about you. However, obsession and addiction affect numerous people, and their impact on me is real.

My goal in this story is to take you behind the scenes into a time of addiction and obsession, showing how these two terms are alike but ultimately distinct. It's almost like a game of tag within your entire being.

Now, that being said, is this story fiction or non-fiction? Please don't over-interpret. The true addict and/or the truly obsessed knows only by living it. I believe every human has an addiction and obsession one in the same to some degree.

Defined:

Obsession: According to the Psychology Dictionary, fixation refers to a persistent attachment to an object or idea, often resistant to attempts to modify it. Psychology Tips explains that obsessive love is an overwhelming desire to possess another person, highlighting the depth of emotional attachment involved.

Addiction: Defined by psychology professionals, addition is a neuropsychological disorder characterized by a persistent and intense urge to use a drug or engage in a behavior that produces a natural reward, despite substantial harm and other negative consequences (Wikipedia).

So, which is it? An obsession or an addiction? Let's go inside the head of an addict and/or one who is obsessed. It's so dark in here, but light when looking out. There is beauty in this place, but darkness covers everything. You can't see it, but it's real. You can't hear it, but it controls your every move. You don't even know what's going on in here. We are just living and thinking everything is great, and we are doing okay.

My addiction is my obsession. I am addicted to weaving words together and obsessed with creating a story that will make a difference in humanity. These stories release some type of intoxicating drug in my mind that brings me a great peace and harmony in my soul that surpasses any drug or drink I've ever had. You may be thinking that my addiction is a wonderful and admirable one to have. I will beg to differ because it takes up twenty hours a day of my mind and has no boundaries of ideas. It's all consuming and forever looking for the next sentence and the next word for the story.

I've asked God to take my sight so many times, but ultimately, that would lead me to be trapped in my mind with memories of a lifetime to write about.

I'm an addict and one who is obsessed with my addiction. I know that statement may not make any physiological sense, but this is true. The definitions mentioned earlier suggest that one is some type of disorder that seeks to engage in behavior that has negative consequences, and the other suggests that there is a preoccupation of the mind that eventually will cause a negative effect on my life.

The problem is that in our society, we love to label everything. We live to label and identify the invisible and what we really don't understand. We include a label to identify these invisible entities and then think we can understand them and draw some type of conclusion about them.

I want to take you on a journey in my life for the day. I want you to understand how this obsession with my addiction impacts me and those who are involved in my life.

Here we go. Waking up at two or three in the morning, listening to that voice in my head. Yes, there is a voice that is speaking to me, but unfortunately, I am the only one who hears it. It is speaking ever so softly of what the day ahead is going to look like. What and how are we going to feed this addiction, and how is the obsession going to help us complete our goal?

If you haven't noticed by now, there are more than one in this psychological warfare. Here is the problem: we don't know we have a problem.

I try to go back to sleep, and sometimes I am successful. I feel the best in the morning when I go back to sleep. Either way, the day goes on. Waking up early, I roll out of the bed, and before I can even see the sunlight, obsession is speaking and addiction is driving me into the place I may or may not want to be. It's a slow and dark place at times; so many emotions and tears are in this place. Sometimes I want to go and sometimes I fight it. Today, I choose to fight! I know I won't win, but I still tell myself it will be different.

Time is so valuable here. I do everything I can do to convince myself otherwise. The morning proceeds either with or without me; time doesn't care about me. It goes on. I am trying to process these emotions that I know will hit hard, and I wonder if I will be able to connect with time and with those who care about me today. Will I be able to see these words come to life? Will I be able to put together a full sentence? It's already noon, and the voices of my addiction and the obsession I have are screaming at me now.

Will I give in? Of course, I will. I'm an addict, and I am obsessed with this addiction. I am who the liar says I am. I have given into the lie of who I am and the reality of how we perceive ourselves. This brings great sadness to my soul because I know I am better than this. I know I am not the lie that is now my reality. Good or bad, an addict is an addict, and we are obsessed with that.

As I move into the evening, the struggle becomes more intense. By now I have worked all day to get to this place. It's either a place of release, peace, solace, grace, mercy, and love, or a place of darkness, sad emotions, confusion, and a constant fight within my mind. This battle is so real that only death can truly separate me from my internal struggle.

Finally, I sit, and it all comes out. Even when I don't see it, it comes out; the words turn to light, the page turns, and the words come to life. There seems to be a real pull-down heaven screen working in the background. The broken come to life in this moment. I come to life in this moment! The life of addiction and obsession is *where you go, I will go, and what you say, I will say.*

The life of an addict is one obsessed with a lie; it's the life of all of us who struggle every day with who we are and what we are doing. Are we all one and the same? Our identity is the lie that we have adopted. Which do we choose on any given day? The lie or the reality? Is it a lie? Where you go I go, what you say I say.

Are we the depressed, the junkie, the fake influencer, the one step from ending it all, the downtrodden, the poor, and the helpless, or are we who God says we are? God, who chased down our hearts, despite all of our failures, and gave us life? A life of purpose, a life of joy, and a life of addiction and obsession with Him! Once lost but now found; I'm not so certain.

We are designed by God to be obsessed and addicted to something. Yes, He designed us to be that way! Like it or not, that is who we are. This world has so many varieties of lies and realities. So many addictions and so many things to bring obsessions to us. Which do we choose? Are we broken into pieces or do we think we are all together?

I fall short so many times, even in my own writings. I am obsessed and addicted to my own words as they come to life on these pages, constantly thinking about what I am going to put on paper today. What is next and how is that next sentence going to make a difference? I struggle to put my God in the front of all my words. I may win this time, but I know I will fail and that's okay. There is a sea of mercy and grace that covers EVERYTHING!

We all struggle with these obsessive addictions; there is so much noise in this world and some noise is louder than others. With that said, some addictions are stronger, and the obsessions take the lives of those in the hardest struggle. I have so many friends who didn't make it. Their addiction and obsession took them. I believe it wasn't their choice but the lie that they believed. Those of us now in the struggle need to be a voice to those who are still alive.

No matter what your addiction and obsession is, there is always hope. Let Hope Rise in humanity—we will make it! There are those that can testify far greater than me to this Glory!

We are designed to be obsessed and addicted to Jesus! I wish it was that easy! It's the scandal of grace so that my soul will live. You are my addiction and obsession forever, and my hope is in you, Jesus!

We live and write for those who don't know yet.

Room Six

This Inn is a one-of-a-kind place. It's where dreams are kept and where peace is found. It's where memories are made and relived. It's where time stands still and your mind finds solace.

It's nestled right on the banks of the Cape Fear River in a small, beautiful North Carolina town. It only has eight rooms, each with its own charm. Six of the rooms have a semi-private porch divided by some wooden slats that go almost to the ground. The old wooden porch swing is my favorite. Each of the riverside rooms has one. They still use keys for the rooms.

This quaint place is named The Riverside Motel.

This time we stayed in room number six for the entire week. Upon arrival, we were greeted by our host who told us, "If you need something, just call me. The keys are on the table in the room."

We were unloading the car for what seemed like an eternity. I complained as usual, and Lisa just looked at me and smiled. As the event continued, other thoughts began to unpack in my mind. I wondered who was staying in room five or room seven. These are all the things I think about when staying in an inn. I think if you played the song, "Hotel California" by Eagles, it would match the Inn. As the song says, "you can check out, but you can never leave."

As we were finishing the unloading process, the door to room seven opened, and a younger couple emerged. They looked like they were in their forties. I made eye contact, and I shook hands with my eyes. Only a few people will ever get this. It's a silent gift that some have. You can have a complete conversation with just your eyes, and we did. It went like this to the both of them, "Hello, how are you? You're in seven, and we are in six. Good to meet you; we can chat later...then blink.

Well, wouldn't you know it. I got sick that week and was unable to do anything. So, while Lisa went to walk each day, I sat on the old porch swing and enjoyed that breeze that came off the river from the ocean. I was working on a previous story titled, "Oh Snap." It's what I call a dark story, but it has a hopeful ending. As I pressed through it, I realized that room seven was out on their porch. They were extremely quiet, not conversing much.

I mustered up enough strength to get to the swing each day to focus and write the story I was working on. I usually wear headphones and listen to what I call my *writing music,* but for some reason, I decided to listen to the peaceful sounds of nature. The swing would rock back and forth and back and forth. I had my laptop out, writing what I thought was a masterpiece. I laugh at myself, saying that because each story I write is not for you but for me; it's a release of emotions that brings healing to me every time. In the back of my mind, I hope these stories will help someone.

Lisa had gone on another long walk about midday. I was in the swing writing and enjoying the sun, and then I heard the door to room seven open and close. I heard the lady talking on the phone. The man was already sitting on the porch. I could see his feet dangling. I couldn't make out what she was saying other than, "Are you sure? Are you one hundred percent?"

The wind had silence in it, as if I was supposed to hear something. There were no boats, no people, no birds, no nothing, just her saying, "Are you sure?" She told the caller, "Okay."

There was silence like I've never heard. I was still trying to focus on the actual story I was fully involved in. It was so difficult to focus. She then told her husband, "The test results are in, and I am terminal. The cancer has taken a turn, and there is no hope of recovery; I am terminal. I have two weeks to live." She joined him on the swing, both feet dangling in the sun, barely touching the ground. They pushed back and forth and back and forth.

He got up and walked into the yard by the river, looking up as if he was asking God Himself for help. I could see the distress in his countenance. She joined him with a beautiful hug in the sunlight as to say, *it's going to be okay. We're going to be ok.* They both started to walk back to room seven, and our eyes took yet another handshake. *It's going to be ok,* I said. *You are going to make it; I promise you that.* Never underestimate the power of the eyes, the look, the glance, the stare, the hug, the kiss, and the touch. It's all real and it brings comfort. They knew what I was saying; they understood. I had overheard a conversation that wasn't meant for me, but it now involved me.

Later that evening, Lisa and I were swinging on that old porch swing in room six, overlooking the Cape Fear River. I had not told her what I had heard earlier that day, as I was still processing everything. Lisa is a cancer survivor, so this is a very sensitive topic for her. I had finished writing my story and shared it with her. She always gives great insight into my stories, and as we chatted about the story, it led to a very common conversation for us.

We started talking about what we always talk about, things of life. As we stared at the stars in the heavens and the waters all around us, we talked about God; we talked about Jesus and the peace and life He brings to us every day. We talked about the plans He has for us, and the future He has for us. We talked about how His amazing grace brought us from where we were to where we are today. We talked about His saving grace and why we are who we are. This is a regular conversation for us.

I then shared with her what I had heard from room seven. Lisa was so torn; she wanted to go over and pray with them to bring some hope and some type of rescue to them but realized this was their battle. If they needed to include us, then only God would make that happen. We agreed to pray right then and there for them. We prayed out loud on that porch swing outside room six for those in room seven. PLEASE GOD HAVE MERCY ON THEM. MAY YOUR WILL BE DONE. IF THEY DON'T KNOW YOU, THEN LEAD THOSE THAT WILL SHOW THEM THE WAY. AMEN.

With that, we went to bed that evening, not sleeping too much. I was feeling better the next day and got up a bit early. I noticed that room seven was packing up the car and preparing to leave. At the Riverside, it's not unusual to have both the front and back doors open at the same time. As I stood in my doorway with my sweet Lisa by my side, we all shook hands again with our eyes. Saying to them, *we love you; it's going to be okay. We will be here if you need us and, most importantly, we love you!*

Not knowing who they were, we often included them in our prayers. A year has passed now, and we are back for our annual vacation time, a celebration of our love and our restoration. I'll include that in another story.

This year, as it happened, we were staying in room six. We were unloading, and in the back of our minds, we were wondering about room seven. We got all settled in. The sun was bright, and the wind was blowing ever so softly.

I peered over to the porch at room seven and noted it was empty. Then I heard a door close. I rushed back to my place on the porch, sitting on the swing, hoping that room seven was occupied.

A man came out and sat on the swing. I could see his feet moving back and forth. He started talking to someone. I was wondering if it was him and hoping that the doctors were wrong.

I stopped, got up quietly, and walked out into the yard toward the river. A voice came from room seven's porch. I turned and it was him. He greeted me with a very soft, "Hello." I returned the greeting. He just stared at me as if to say something and finally said, "You were here last year about this time, right?"

I said, "Yes, we were." I didn't act dumb; I knew she didn't make it.

We made it past the introductions, and he told me the whole story about her cancer, her diagnosis, and the final two weeks of her life. Our eyes engaged, and once again, we communicated in silence. He then said, "I have a letter here for you. She wrote it and sealed it up before she passed, with the hopes of me one day seeing you again to deliver it."

And the letter read:

> Dear Room Six,
>
> I know we only shook hands with our eyes, but I overheard you and your sweet Lisa, as you called her, talking. I heard you talking about this God and this Jesus that brings peace and hope to your souls. I did hear you talking about a life everlasting and a life in this place called heaven. I wanted you to know that in the last two weeks of my life, God has brought some amazing people into my life. They have shared with me this love of Jesus. I overheard you *room six*, and I

am thankful that I did. Thanks to you, *room six*, my husband now understands and has this same hope.

He knows God's plan for him is to prosper and not harm him. He knows his future is even brighter with this everlasting love. If you are reading this now, you know I overheard. For that, I am grateful beyond words. See you soon!

Signed,

Room Seven

With that, you never know the power of the spoken word. Choose wisely.

DON'T GIVE
UP
GOD IS
WITH YOU

A Tale Of Souls Cities

Greetings from Souls City, the haven for the lost and forgotten. We've dwelled here for ages, and I am the spokesman, your point of contact from here on out. If you attempt to breach our realm, even by familial ties, you may be banned from any future contacts.

We comprise a tight-knit colony of lost souls, often questioned about our purpose. Our mission is to collect the forgotten of the two cities. Some call us the trash collectors of sorts. Are these souls truly discardable refuse? To some, perhaps. Yet they are more than just trash; they are the overlooked and the disregarded. Our task is to gather those souls who are lost and forgotten. Who decides their status? Some say it's humanity, but others would say fate. But regardless, our duty is to rescue these souls.

There are those who say there is another city that collects the righteous and the ones who are called to a purpose and have hope. I've asked about this place, and I haven't received a conformation that this city exists. I believe it does. I'm considering venturing out of my city limits to conduct a more comprehensive investigation. As I have mentioned before, I am the spokesman for Souls City, so it seems fitting that I would be the one to deliver any news of a potential *tale of two cities* to the community.

So, with that being said, I pack up and gather my tools and supplies to make the trip. Souls City is a desolate land; there is no green grass, no green trees, and no colors of any kind; It's just black and white. That defines our position in humanity. We are lost in color, and only think in yes or no. There is no gray here. Our minds are bound to the present, and there is a limited vocabulary. There are several words that are foreign in our land and one of them is hope. Souls City is devoid of hope, and that's okay for now. We have dwelt in hopelessness for years, and that doesn't seem to bother anyone here. So why change?

Finally, I'm all packed up. I have everything I need to make this exploration. There are a handful of souls here to see me off. In the depths of their being, I sense a yearning for me to return with the story of a city overflowing with promise.

A city that is hopeful and a city that brings life to humanity. In the deepest part of my being, I desire this as well. That's the purpose of my exploration.

I take my first steps toward the unknown. You don't need much when you have no hope. All you need is a little of this and a little of that. When there is no hope and no promise of tomorrow, it doesn't take much to transport you to the next place.

I've been walking this path for days now, and I still haven't found a city of hope. I've traveled east and west. I've been north and south, but still no sign of a new city. The land here is as barren as the North Sea. There is nothing but wave after wave of hopelessness. I thought I knew what an absence of hope was until this exploration. I mentioned that *hope* is not a word in Souls City, but that doesn't mean we don't know about it.

After several months, I still see no trace of this city some claim exists. At this point, I haven't surrendered hope—not that I had much to lose to begin with. How long is this going to take? I wasn't sure, but it really doesn't matter at this point, anyway. Even finding my way back seems improbable.

I am in a land that is so desperate that the sand makes conversation to stay in existence.

Years have elapsed since then. The count eludes me, yet I know my absence isn't consequential to those in Souls City. Well, perhaps a few of those souls might be on the lookout for me, though that's likely my hopelessness speaking. As the years have passed, I have persisted day by day and week by week, searching for that elusive city that might bring hope. If such a place exists, perhaps they know the location of Souls City and can point me back in that direction. I am not only lost, but completely dead to myself. Some may deem it hopeless, but to me, it's simply life.

As I look ahead, about to take what seems like my last breath, I notice something in the distance. Step after step, day after day, I have inched closer to this city's edge. I collapse by the sign that reads, "Hopeful City – Where Lives Are Changed and Grace is Given Freely." I found it! I found it! Tears stream down my face and flood my soul. Is this real? Hope flows into my soul, bringing new life into my weary body, just from reading the sign at the city limits. I am exhausted and crushed but given new life at this moment.

I have found this new city—a place of stories woven with grace and mercy, a haven of hope. Its inhabitants rush out to meet me, eager to know where I have traveled from. My answer is simple. "I've traveled a long distance over many years from a place devoid of hope. That place, Souls City, needs you all. They live in a city that doesn't have hope." They recognized the name of the city; its where they all came from many years ago. With that, they all band together and load up to make a trip back to Souls City to share with the people the reason for their hope.

So, it turns out the tale of two cities is true. There is hope through mercy and grace. While they may appear parallel in nature, only one focuses on the vertical dimension. In this vertical alignment, we discover the source of hope, mercy, and grace.

5-10-25
U.S.
COINS
ONLY
50¢
6 Min.

Oh Snap

Oh snap! Before I knew it, I found myself at the bottom of a pit. It happened overnight, leaving me bewildered. I hadn't experienced that feeling in several years. There was no tail spin or spiral; I simply woke up to find myself in a pit of despair.

I was not just exhausted; I was in a place that I could only hope to emerge from once again. It's a constant battle to break free from this place. If you've been there, you know what I'm talking about.

As I looked around in this dark pit, I noticed it was a cylinder about six feet in circumference, and the walls were made of a type of dark, slippery mud. The mud was streaming down the pit, and I knew it was going to be a struggle to get to the top. Could I make it out? I wasn't sure this time.

I glanced upwards, searching for any sign of light, and there, in the distance, a dim light flickered. It felt incredibly far away, almost unreachable. I felt lost, my heart heavy with pain, uncertain if I would survive. My head just sunk and my eyes closed, questioning the impact of this evil and the weight of my human emotions. Will I even live?

Lisa saw something in me early that morning and asked me if I was okay. I assured her I was just fine. In my heart, I believed God's love was giving me the will to survive. My only hope was in my redeemer, trusting that

I would come out of this dark and lonely place. I know His name holds power and can break any stronghold.

The walls were so thick and the climb out would be one of the most difficult of all time. For the past two and a half years, I've been equipped with the tools to face the walls of this darkness.

Lisa continued to press me for clarity, checking in with me hour by hour. It became increasingly frustrating, not just navigating out of the pit but also seeing the love of my life trying to rescue me from it. She understood where I was; she has a special way about her. She threw me a lifeline in the pit, but I couldn't see it—it was too dark.

Has anyone reading this ever experienced a similar place of despair? I was in pain, but I knew I was not alone in the pit. I knew that there was another presence with me in the darkness.

As the hours passed during that day, it seemed I was living a dual life. A life of despair and a life of hope. As I grabbed the lifeline of hope and spoke the name of Jesus, I slowly made my way out of this pit of the strongholds that had held me captive.

The darkness had not prevailed that time. Lisa asked me one more time if I was okay. My answer was very simple, "I am." I told her about the intense battle I had faced within myself that day, in a pit deeper than any I had ever known. She understood and explained she had been praying for me.

She prayed I could break every stronghold and emerge victorious! That I did! As the power, known to only a few, lifted me out of the pit, I didn't struggle to reach the top but emerged victorious, not by my own strength, but by the power of Jesus. These broken pieces, buried deep in the pit, were brought to life by a light I hope you can also find, as I did.

I need to be real with you here; it was never me, but Him. I have been given invaluable tools by a remarkable person who understands humans like no one I have ever known. She perceives every thought and its impact on my emotional well-being. With her guidance, I've learned to navigate the exhaustion, stress, and pain of life. Coupled with the faith that anchors me, everything falls into place. It's a delicate balance between faith and human emotions. And then there's my sweet Lisa, a wonderful and beautiful lifeline who recognized the pit I was in, prayed for me, and encouraged me throughout my darkest hours.

Coming out of the pit is never easy; it never becomes easy. It is far simpler to fall into it, given our human nature. Our thoughts, emotions, and our spirit must be guarded constantly. Keep looking up; that's where you will find hope, and HIS grace will restore all the broken pieces.

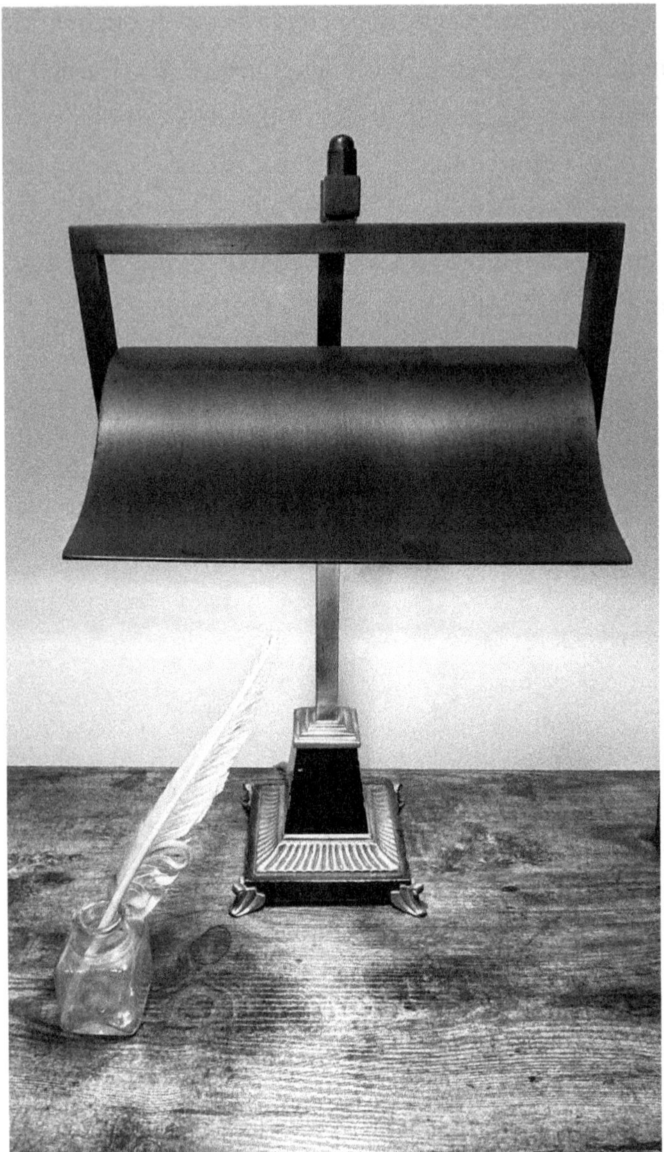

The Writers Museum

She visited the museum every day, consistently making her way to my exhibit. Sometimes, she brought friends along, purposely guiding them past me, almost as if she was showing me off. Her beauty was striking, with long brown hair and captivating brown eyes that matched her elegant style. Her presence in the museum was intoxicating, like a gentle breeze that enchanted everyone who saw her.

It was natural for her to come to the museum; after all, she was a talented writer herself. This museum was dedicated to writers, showcasing both the renowned and lesser-known ones; each exhibit was beautifully crafted for each time period.

Allow me to introduce myself. My name is Harry Fawnsworth, and I am an exhibit in this museum. The year is 1817, and I just finished a novel titled "Lisa," a romantic book that reflects the love of my life. My exhibit is set in a charming wood-laden library that houses all the books of the past centuries. The writer's desk I occupy is a hand-carved oak piece, surrounded by scattered pages longing for words that elude me. Soft lighting envelops my exhibit, adding a touch of realism to this time period.

I'm dressed in an eloquent black suit paired with a crisp white shirt. My shoes gleam with shiny black leather, matching the hue of my hat. My skin is tan because I loved to sit outside and write. I have a meticulously styled handlebar mustache, waxed up to impress the ladies and make the men jealous. I hold a beautiful writing instrument in my hand that was invented during this century.

Every day, she stops and stares at me. For hours, she watches me with great intent. I want to speak to her, but I am unable. She's in the early 1900s, enjoying a progressive era in America. She revels in a life of peace and prosperity. What could I possibly offer her? My hands don't move, and my speech is confined to the contents of my exhibit. I just sit here day after day, trapped in my realm. Oh, did I mention I am in a different dimension?

This writer's museum is different from any other museum. We, as writers, can perceive each other and communicate indirectly, almost as if in another dimension. We observe and comprehend your conversations and written expressions. Occasionally, we have been able to communicate our thoughts to the paper on our desk. So how does that work you may ask? The mechanics behind this phenomenon are a mystery to us; it happens spontaneously and without explanation. It's a rare occurrence, yet it happens.

Day after day, this beautiful lady comes in. Recently, she even engaged me in conversation; I could hardly hear her because she spoke so softly. She sways back and forth, coming close to breaching the red velvet ropes that surround me. I can smell the beauty in her hair and in her melodious voice. One day, she leaned in so close that a slight breeze caused strands of her hair to brush against my face.

That's when it happened. My words in my mind came to life on the paper right under my pen. It was a simple thought that appeared on the paper: "You are so beautiful. Please join me. Signed, Harry."

She looked down at the paper and couldn't conceal her shock. It was as if she was frozen for a moment and couldn't speak or move. She was paralyzed. *Oh my*, I thought. *What have I done*? After a few moments, she dashed out of the museum. I was as heartbroken as the novel that I had just completed. It seemed to end the same way; she just ran away.

I looked for her every day; we all did. All of us writers, regardless of our era, rallied around this marvelous story that was being written in real life. Day after day and week after week, there was no sign of her. Was she gone forever?

Then one day, the door to the museum opened; I looked with determination, and it was her. My heart jumped, and my mind was free from the costly mistake I had made, even though it was not my intent but the powerful thought of love I have for this stunning lady. She made her way down that long hallway toward my exhibit, each step deliberate and calculated. As she approached, I could see her scanning the paper below my pen, and the words were still there. Right below my hand were new words, and they read, "I'm sorry." They had appeared on the paper weeks after she left me. She read them and seemed unfazed. The other writers in the museum watched in awe as this romance unfolded right before them. Was it truly possible to bring another to our world like this?

She stood there and stared at me for hours. I dared not dwell too deeply on our connection, knowing that each thought could bring new words to the pages in front of me. I could not make the same mistake. I could see her lips moving as she was speaking to me, but not so loudly that I or anyone else could hear her. She left after a few hours and would return day after day, just like in the past.

Once more, she entered the room. A lanyard hung around her neck from a recent writers' convention held next door. We were all aware of the convention, which brought in fledgling authors, sharing their words, dreams, and visions. These writers discussed their stories and the impact their words would have on humanity.

As she drew closer to me, I could read her badge. Her name was Lisa. *Oh my*, I thought. *Was she the one who had left me in the last novel I wrote in 1817?* There she was—a bombshell wrapped in mystery. What was her last name? You guessed it, *Fawnsworth*. Who was this exquisite lady? Had she escaped this dimension somehow and left the pages of my last novel in sadness?

It was her. My sweet Lisa had somehow escaped the pages of my very last novel before I passed. It wasn't supposed to end that way, but somehow it had to because she was gone. Now, she is found. I can see the love in her eyes—the great salvation that she brings to life, mending the broken. She has brought me to an excitement for life, even in my dimension. There is hope that we can finish the novel with a proper ending. Even though it's a hundred years later. Is she willing? I'm just not sure.

Once lost, but now found. I've been blind, but now I can envision this beauty in front of me.

My sweet Lisa continued to return day after day and watch me and the paper beneath my hands, waiting for a message. A sign to come back, a signal to return to her love.

One day the curator of the museum placed an empty chair right beside me. I wasn't sure why or what he was doing. He was acting as if I needed a new addition to the exhibit. This frustrated me, but I had no say in the matter because I was just an exhibit; I was honored to be in the mist of the best writers in the world. That empty chair stayed that way for months.

Lisa continued to visit day after day, and I could see she was perplexed by the empty chair as well. Because of my frustration, the words just appeared on the pages in front of me and they inked, "Will you join me, Lisa?" *Oh my, what will she think when she comes in today? Will she run again? Will she never return?* It was time; it's been long enough. She will either join me or never raise to life this story that needs to end the right way.

She appears—a picture of amazing grace and exquisite beauty. She is void of judgment, unyielding in her love, and always accepting those full of fault. She looks at the chair and then looks at the page in front of me and sees the words, "Will you join me, Lisa?"

She speaks in a gentle voice, but I can't understand her. She steps over the red velvet rope beside me, places her hand on mine, and says, "Yes, I will join you." She sits beside me in the chair.

The pages come to life now, speaking all the words of grace that abound. I've laid myself down to bring the broken to life. Lisa is back now, and she now knows that His grace is sufficient. How sweet the sound of what is now being written. As she sits beside me, she comes to the dimension of grace and love. The place where she is going and where she belongs. She's been set free.

It's the writer's museum where stories are written every day and where the lost are found and new beginnings start. Come by and visit. That empty chair might change your life. Will you sit?

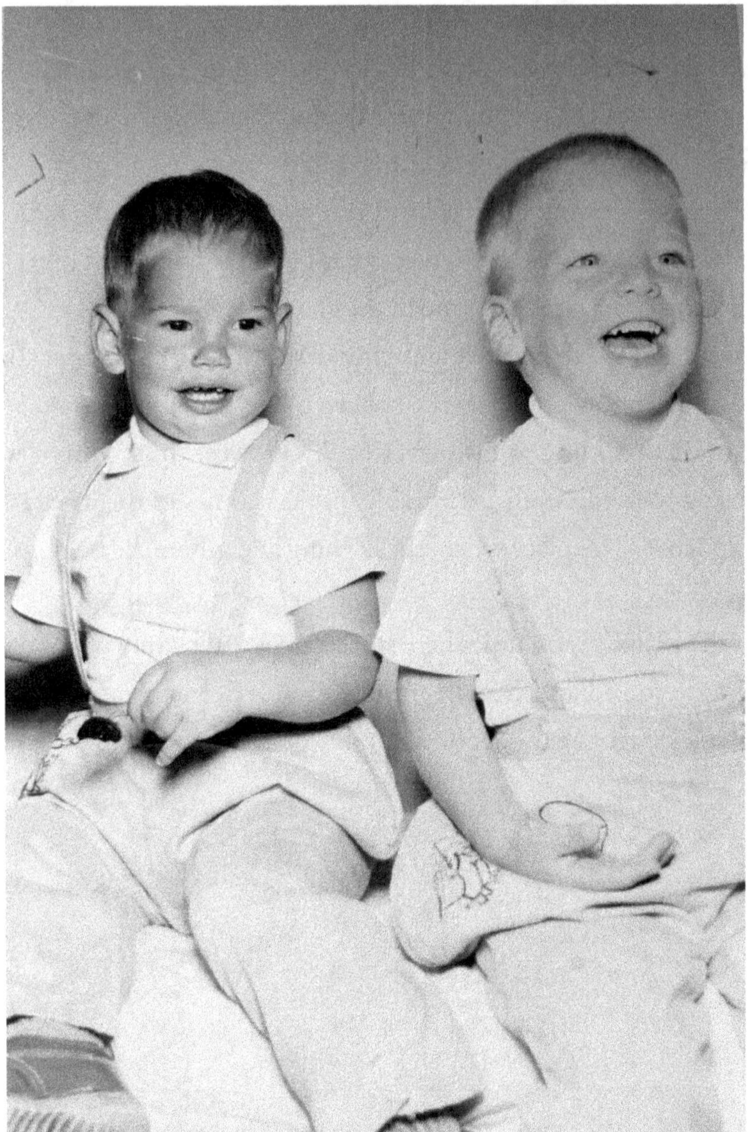

Was It Love or Was It...

According to Wikipedia, **betrayal** is defined as "the breaking or violation of a presumptive contract, trust, or confidence that produces moral and psychological conflict within a relationship amongst individuals."

Is this a story of betrayal or the story of a mother wanting to save the life of her son? You be the judge.

At the age of five, I trailed behind a group of individuals, accompanied by my mom and the evil person she had married. We were entering what would be my new residence. I had been removed from my home because of the torture I was enduring by this evil person. Describing the extent of the damage he wrought upon me and my siblings is a challenge; the scars he left run deep, making it difficult to articulate the sheer malevolence he embodied.

I have never given that person the satisfaction of calling him a man or even a step dad. You may feel the emotion in my words even in describing this person, but this story is not about him. It's more about the emotions I've carried around for decades. I've been treading around these waters for a few years now. I've been sticking my toes in, and sometimes I can put my whole foot in. Now I'm about to be waist deep in these waters of betrayal. My hope is that I don't fall in a pit here and sink.

My biological father was absent from my childhood. For most of my life, I've held him responsible for the pain and suffering caused by the poor choices my mom made. He ended his race with a bullet.

I remember entering that giant brick building that I would call home from then on. I met my new mother and all my new brothers. "This is George," she screamed to the entire house. As I stood at the door with my paper bag of clothes, I watched my mom walk away. As my mom and the social worker drove off, I could see her looking back at me. I could see the anguish in her tiny eyes.

I wasn't sure if she would ever come back for me, or if she would make it through her own torture at the hands of this evil person. I could only hope that the evil would die.

I was led to my bed in a row of several other boys. They just looked at me as if I were damaged goods. In truth, we were all in the same boat. None of us had a place to call home. There was no one to give us a hug, no one to crease our hair, and no one to say the words, "I love you." We were all isolated in our own little worlds. Even at five, we were all trying to understand why we were betrayed. Or were we?

It wasn't until recently that I realized the deep-seated emotion I had been carrying all along was betrayal. For so long, I harbored feelings of anger, frustration, and resentment towards my mom, feeling there must be something more beneath the surface. Despite knowing about forgiveness and surrendering to God's will, I still felt a profound sense of confusion about this aspect of my life.

Now, as I immerse myself in this story, I realize that if I can finish it, I will break free from strongholds that have bound me for decades. This story is unfolding in real time and the emotions that are surfacing are really extraordinary.

We have defined what betrayal is, but what about love? Let's delve into this further.

Love encompasses a range of intense and positive emotional states, ranging from profound virtues and deep interpersonal affection to the simplest pleasure. For example, the love of a mother differs from the love of a spouse, which differs from the love for food. Most commonly, love refers to a feeling of strong attraction and emotional attachment.

People consider love to be both positive and negative, with its virtue representing human kindness, compassion, and affection—defined as "the unselfish, loyal and benevolent concern for the good of another" (Wikipedia).

After reading this definition, I find my heart overflowing with love for my mom. Suddenly, the fear, depression, anger, disgust, and resentment I felt for her for just disappear. The betrayal I had carried with me for so many years now seems insignificant. The last sentence in the definition says it all. She demonstrated love in an unselfish and loyal way, and her concern was for my well-being. It's clear to me now that she was never solely focused on herself. She wanted to save me and give me the best chance at life that I could have, and for that I am forever grateful.

Is it possible to feel betrayed and deeply loved but not know it? I'm not talking about something that happened last year or a few years ago; this happened decades ago, and it's one of my first memories. For most of my life, I've had a profound lack of trust and confidence in others. I never knew she loved me that much. Identifying with the betrayal was so easy for so many years. But as I write this, I realize it wasn't betrayal at all—it was an act of love, a desperate attempt to rescue me from the death that was sure to come.

Now that's she's gone, there is no opportunity to express my gratitude. No chance to embrace her, kiss her, or explain to her that her child has overcome this deep-seated emotion of betrayal. I can only lift my eyes to the heavens on this moonlit night and cry out to her, screaming, "I love you."

It reminds me of the song, *Scandal of Grace*. (Hillsong)

Too much to make sense of it all
I know that Your love breaks my fall
The scandal of grace
You died in my place
So my soul will live

Her motive will always be a scandal of grace. I am now free from this emotion of betrayal and full of the grace of her love.

The song reminds us that the true scandal of grace brings true life to our soul that this world wants to destroy,

All to be like You
Give all I have just to know You
Jesus, there's no one beside You
Forever the hope in my heart

Now, the story goes on. I'm now walking out of this river of water that has surrounded me for so many years, and now I've been washed and baptized in the truth that has set me free. It was out of love! Forever, Mom, you brought hope to my heart. I love you, Mom!

Jeremiah 29:11
New Living Translation

11 *For I know the plans I have for you," says the Lord. "They are plans for good and not for disaster, to give you a future and a hope.*

Black Creek

As we all grew into our mid-teens, we experienced new and exciting things. Every day was a new adventure for us, especially in the summer. During the carefree days of summer, we created some of the greatest memories of all times. This is one of those memories.

It was extremely hot that year, hotter than it had ever been before. That summer was one of the hottest on record. Because the lake was shallow, it felt like a warm tub. We couldn't escape the heat that summer, so we headed down to Bella Coola.

Bella Coola was the name of the road that took us to the back side of the lake where there were creeks that flowed into the lake. The creeks never seemed to move; the water just stood still.

The water was so dark, and the unknowns were real. It's funny looking back now; the snakes and alligators never seemed to bother us. We just tried to make sure they knew we were there.

Black Creek was our destination. The water was cool, black, and deep. There was just enough room to pull our cars over in the tall grass before arriving at the bridge. The silver guardrail on the bridge was flattened by people who had been there before us, and their names were carved into the thick, painted surface. Ours were too by then. We had earned our right to put our names on that rail. Anyone who would swim there deserved the honor.

At any time, there were two or twenty of us swimming at that hole. One thing was for sure; if we were first on the scene, we always picked up a large rock and threw it in. This was to announce our arrival to the snakes and alligators. The first one in was a dare thing, "You go first, no you go, no you go." Once we saw that person make it to shore with all their limbs, we figured it was clear.

One game we loved to play was *underwater tag*. The water was so dark you couldn't see anything once you went under a foot or two. To get tagged, you had to be under water; the rules were the name of the game. I would always shoot for the bottom, grabbing a log or something that was sticking up from the bottom. I would sit there in the dark water, wondering what was near me. Every now and then, something would tickle my leg or back, and I would swim to the top of the water. Then I would run up the shore to the top of the bridge, screaming, "Snake! Alligator!" We all would clear out and jump in again, laughing so hard we would almost lose our breath.

One thing about Black Creek, it brought out the best in us. Want to know why? Even though it may seem stupid to swim where you know the snakes and alligators live and where you can't see through the murky darkness of the water, this journey represents our life.

We live with the snakes and alligators of life every day. We live in the unknown of what's next, and if you know Jesus Christ, there is never darkness. As with Black Creek, there may be dark times, but someday you will surface to the top victorious. You will surface screaming, "I made it! I made it! I made it!" You will live to tell others your story of the Black Creek you swam through.

One more thing about Black Creek I need to mention—it's quiet and lonely in the darkness. When you're under the water about ten feet down, there is nothing but stillness. No sound, no light, and no hope of being found. So, the question to you is, "Are you in Black Creek?"

If you are, there is always hope! Hope in Jesus Christ. Don't let Satan keep you under that deep, dark water. It will kill you, and that is what he wants to do!

> 1 Timothy 1:15-19 (MSG) "Here's a word you can take to heart and depend on: Jesus Christ came into the world to save sinners. I'm proof—Public Sinner Number One—of someone who could never have made it apart from sheer mercy. And now he shows me off—evidence of his endless patience—to those who are right on the edge of trusting him forever."

Fight to swim to the top. Fight to get up that hill. Fight to get back on that bridge and jump for joy when you reach the top. Thank God for His mercy, and by His grace, we will make it. By His mercy, we will stand and prepare for another amazing adventure.

Teardrops

I'm sitting here watching the lake today. It's a beautiful day; the sun is shining so brightly, and the wind is very soft. With every bright day, there is always a chance a storm will pop up. Suddenly, the wind shifts direction, gaining strength, and I observe the clouds swiftly advancing over this picturesque lake. I can see the storm brewing in the back side of these clouds. The clouds are getting darker and darker, and they are twisting in and out as if they are playing with each other.

As the storm draws closer, I retreat from my seat on the deck into the screened-in porch. Standing with my arms crossed, I am mesmerized by this beautiful storm. It's more enchanting than words can describe. I've never seen a storm like this before. You know all storms are different in the countless eyes of humanity.

The storm now approaches land, and I notice the wind has a calming effect to it. Then the beauty comes. The clouds are now darker than ever, and they are rolling like waves in the ocean. I can hear them rumble. As I step closer to the screen on the porch, I observe something that is falling out of the sky; it resembles rain, but it's not wet.

Transparent, tear-shaped drops fall gently to the ground as if they are waiting to be caught. Some are as large as pears, and some as small as garden peas. I see them hitting the ground, but they just disappear.

I want to open the screen door, but I'm not sure if it's safe. Larger drops, now clear, float by, inviting discovery. The smaller ones require me to be closer than I am comfortable.

I can see it now. These are drops of memories and emotions, each with a story to tell. As I study them closer in my safe place on the porch, I notice each drop has an emotion to release. Am I safe now? I'm not sure.

I'm drawn to this storm for some reason; I feel compelled to step out in it, but I don't right away. The pull is getting stronger, and the force is beginning to pull me.

The storm intensifies, and I am drawn outside, surrendering to its beauty and the memories it unveils. I'm no longer fearful of this storm, but now embrace these emotions and memories.

In the grass, I see emotions and memories in teardrop form, wanting to escape their prison. The larger drops are floating ever so closely to me. They are not speaking, but they are replaying the emotion and the memory that was blind but now seen. This storm has brought a title wave of these emotions and memories. It's so clear to me now; it is safe for me to see these now.

The trees are now swaying back and forth, the wind is picking up, and these emotions and memories are circling around me more. They want to be discovered and released from their teardrop form. They have been trapped in this prison for so many years. I've never really noticed what was falling to the ground until today when I took the time to watch the approaching storm.

The storm uncovers what was trampled, kicked, and covered up for years. The larger drops swirl around me in a twister like fashion, causing the drops on the ground to come to life. In the vortex, I feel safe capturing each story of grace, redemption, and my place in humanity.

Some may not understand, and that's okay; your storm has not come across the lake just yet. When it does, don't be afraid to step out and examine each teardrop as it falls. Don't miss the grace that has been given to you; it's where I used to be.

There is another in the storm that is next to you. You can hear him if you listen. Don't be afraid to leave those drops on the ground; some are meant for harm, but all have a place in your life. They are part of the totality of the storm.

I'm crying, but there are no tears; no one sees and does anyone really care? Can you see there are no tears on this little boy's face? Why do you say he's sad or in pain? Can it be possible to cry inside where no one ever sees? It's possible!

For those whose storm is on the way, take shelter, wait for safety, and remember the purpose in each drop. The storm that brings destruction becomes a beautiful storm of life, breaking strongholds, and bringing peace into your life. All these drops in the vortex of this twister can move us all into healing and bring a tranquility to life that is more than you can ever imagine.

Acknowledging the storm across the lake wasn't easy, but through life's circumstances, I was ready. Caught up in a vortex, I was lifted to a sky of freedom, peace, and contentment.

I am looking forward to writing out each of these emotions and each memory that goes along with that. Burn like a fire! This world needs you!

Almost Got Away With It

Isaiah 60:22 (MSG) says, "I am God. At the right time I'll make it happen."

It was a hot summer night at Lake Waccamaw, and there wasn't much going on, as usual. We could have walked down to *Dupree Landing* or gone fishing, but this night we did something that would take our summer away and change us all forever.

There were about ten of us, all in our early teens. We weren't looking for trouble, just some fun on a hot summer's night. There were several suggestions thrown out, but none seem to satisfy our inner craving to have fun. So, we took the last request and decided to go with that. We decided we were going to *egg* the first car that came around the corner on Lake Shore Drive. We first needed the key ingredient, and that was eggs. So, we raided the pantry at the cottage, got several dozen, and headed for the lake.

We had our plan mapped out. We were going to hit the car hard and dive into the lake. Then we planned to split up and meet back at the cottage later for the laugh. That poor car came around the corner on Lake Shore Drive, and it sounded like hail was hitting it. We tore that thing up, laughing and running at the same time.

We all hit the lake wide open, and the car didn't stop. You could hear the engine's four barrel kick in; they were out of there and so were we. As we all went our separate ways, Rick and I found ourselves at an old boathouse. We climbed out of the water and made our way back to the cottage. Then, little by little, the rest of the crew showed up.

We were laughing our heads off, carrying on like only wild teenagers could do. We all retired for the evening and had a peaceful night's sleep. We knew we had done something big and gotten away with it.

The next evening, Jim called a meeting with all the guys in the cottage; there were about fifteen of us. He told us that a car had been *egged* at the lake the night before and wanted to know if any of us were involved with that terrible act. Of course, we all said "NO." He gave us several chances to confess, but we all held our ground. Then something crazy happened. He called each of us by name who had been involved with the terrible act. We asked who would have done such a terrible thing. As he lined us all up in front of the other guys, we were still denying what we had done. This didn't seem to sway Jim at all. He had already decided our punishment. He said, "Meet me at the tool shed tomorrow night and every night after that until I say different."

We all hung our head low and went to bed that night. Knowing that we had to pay the price for that few minutes of fun. We all were in disbelief that we got caught, wondering how he knew. Did someone tell? If so, that would have been grounds for *out-casting*. You never told on anyone!

The next evening, we all met at the tool shed and lined up. He was handing out *sling blades* and *chop axes*. He pointed toward the railroad tracks and said, "Start over there and work your way to the east." The tracks went all the way to Wilmington. Well, that summer we chopped grass from six o'clock until dark and then ran a mile. Jim was with us the whole way, telling us we had way too much energy. I remember how hot it was and how thirsty we would get. We could see all the other guys playing on the field, going to the gym, or just sitting around. We were in a place that didn't have bars or a fence but was inescapable.

There was a great deal of talk that summer of running away, but no one ever did. Our hands were full of blisters, our backs were hurting, and we complained to deaf ears. There was an excellent life lesson being taught to all of us and the ones to come behind us. I think this story has made it to the *book of legends*. I can see the boys talking now. "Let's egg a car," and then silence comes around the circle of guys and one speaks up, "You remember the story of those guys back in the day?" There are many of these stories in the *book of legends*. I had heard most of them from my years at the home.

I heard that one of the guys who was with us that night became rich and had those train tracks removed from Lake Waccamaw to Wilmington. I visit the lake from time to time, driving right past the place where we worked so hard to learn a lesson that none of us would ever forget. I can still see us out there. While we worked hard for our mistake, we walked away that summer with a different view of life. If you do something that you shouldn't be doing, there will be a price to pay. It's the law of the land; it's God's law. You reap what you sow, or better put, there are always consequences to your sins.

In the act of doing a bad thing, it was fun, but just for the moment. Later we paid the price! How did Jim know? Only he knows, and to this day, he has not revealed to us who told.

Well, as you can guess, we never even thought about *egging* another car. We learned a great deal about respecting those who knew more than we did. We learned that if we did something wrong, discipline was sure to follow, striping us of our pride and bad attitudes. We learned that there are some things in life we will never know. No matter what you are doing, someone knows about it. This is a great picture of God. He is all knowing.

I think the most important message in this story is when we are in sin, we either deny it or confess it. To deny it means we are too prideful to omit we are wrong. To confess it means we know we are wrong and are willing to correct it. Pride will either take control of your life or you can control it; we all have it to some degree. When it is put into check, God can do more than you could ever imagine. That is a great picture of Jesus on the cross, who died for our sins!

I have thought for days about how I could end this story. There is no right way to end it because it never ended. Most of us involved that night are still alive today and are still living out this story. There were many stories after this one. We just got smarter and wiser, or so we thought!

The Fire

Recently, I was challenged to write a story about someone who must keep a fire burning, surrounded by total darkness. I have been thinking about this for a few days and have been pondering what type of emotions I will have to explore to write this story. This has triggered a host of troubling emotions and thoughts. The darkness in my life has always been real.

The memory that stands out to me is when my brother, Mike, and I were dropped off at this lady's house during the week. She ran some type of off-grid daycare. We were about four or five years old. I believe it was the year before I was removed from my home. Even on our best behavior, we found ourselves in this dark closet. It was in a room that was already dark, and the closet was even darker. No light shined in at all. It was total darkness.

My brother is one year older than me. He sat on one side of the closet, and I sat on the other side. The closet was about four feet wide, and I remember our feet touching the walls with our knees in the bent position. I would always grab my knees and place my head right in the middle of my legs. We would sit there for hours, listening for any sound of hope. We always hoped to be released from the closet early. Some days we would hear footsteps, and the door would open; we would be led out into the light.

Our eyes would be half-closed and our legs would hardly work because we had been sitting so long in one position.

The resilience of the darkness brought many imaginary things to life. We knew the darkness was real, and it provided solace and comfort, but being seen by someone could lead to torture or other forms of abuse. We made the darkness our friend. I couldn't see my brother, but I knew he was there. I would often say, "Mike, are you there?" He always answered in a sweet, small voice, "Yes, I'm here." As I write this, tears are streaming down my face. These emotions are stronger than I had originally thought, but I am going to press on. It's a yellow door situation. I have an escape plan.

As we sat there, hour after hour, we would make up things to do in the darkness. One thing we did most often was to build a fire. One, so we could keep warm because it was cold in that closet, and two, so we could have some light to see each other. We had grown to expect to be put in the closet. We knew going in what we were going to have to do. Mike would often say, "Get the fire going because I'm cold." I would say, "I need some light in here." This was a necessity, not a game. We knew we needed each other, and we needed light. Fire is light. I would imagine what my brother's face looked like and would depend on that image to get me through to the light of day.

When we had the fire going, I would say, "You feel that?" Mike would always say, "Yes, I feel it, George." I fanned the flames more and more, and the light would illuminate his face from his chin to his hairline. "There you are, my brother," I would say. As the flames grew larger, I could see the closet and the contents. There was an old coat and some hangers on a rail just above me. It was mostly empty, except for one thing. There was some writing on the wall about mid-way down the closet. We were not the only ones who had been put in that closet before. There had been generations of innocent children shut up in that darkness. Broken to pieces.

The writing on the wall read, "Keep the fire going; never let it go out. Fan the flames and keep adding wood and you will make it." It was signed in a scripted word that looked like HOPE.

So, my job each day at just four years old was to fan the flames for my brother and me. He was much stronger than me, but I was more technically minded and the only one who could start the fire and keep it going. Even now when we chat, I am the encourager, the one who brings enlightenment, and the one who brings some clarity to any circumstance. His part of handing me the wood to feed the fire was important in that closet. We worked together.

Those who had gone before us had forged a path of hope. It is written in that closet. In the darkness, there is hope; in the light, there is hope; in the midst of any circumstance, there is always hope. No matter if you find yourself in the darkest place on earth, there is light. You have a part to play in the closet—to fan the flames. They may be dim at first, but you will see the writings on the wall signed by HOPE.

Amazing grace is what we can call it. Coming out of that dark closet each day with my little eyes barely opened, I knew there would be more to endure in this life and that was just the beginning. I knew that what I read on that wall was not meant just for me, but for all of us.

My task of writing about someone who had to keep a fire burning, surrounded by total darkness, has become all too real to me. This story opened a floodgate of emotions, but as always, with the release of the thoughts and emotions, I am free. My hope is ever alive, and I know that whatever and wherever you are broken, there is always HOPE! It is written!

So, What Do You See?

We rarely ask our friends or family their opinions on how we could improve our lives. Honestly, we don't really ask people for advice about our lives unless we know what they are going to say. It is a rare thing to ask friends what they think we should do in a particular circumstance.

We are quick to invite help into our lives when we are in our comfort zone of asking. Take waterskiing, for instance. When I'm skiing, I see and feel the things that I am doing wrong or need to improve on. When I get to the end of the course, I usually ask, "What did you see?" You would not believe the responses I get sometimes. If the person was paying attention, he will be sharp and quick to tell me, "Lean more behind the boat; don't pull in with your arms; you're giving up your angle." The list goes on and on. I won't always ask. Sometimes I will just look into the boat with a look of *help me*.

If the person riding in the boat says something like, "Well, I really didn't see anything," then I know he may not have been paying attention to my skiing. This is not a problem, by the way. Sometimes, I prefer when people are not watching me; I can stay focused on my task, and that is simply completing the course. Think about that statement just for a minute, "I prefer it when people are not watching so I can just focus on completing the course."

We don't like people watching us with the intent of giving us advice. This is especially true with our spiritual lives and our family life.

Has anyone ever told you how to raise your child? I have been told, and my response to them was not Christ-like. Has anyone ever told you, "You're wrong in what you are doing: you are hurting the body of Christ with that attitude, and your sin is causing problems?"

That's a tough one, but these are statements we don't often hear. I wonder why that is. I believe it's the fact that some of us are bound by pride; some bound by embarrassment; and some are bound by fear. We may not want to know what others think about our inner lives. This is a very trusted area, and you shouldn't go to everyone asking for their advice. Also, be wary of asking people for advice who have put their lives in tiny boxes and think you are wrong if you step outside of those boundaries. Just use wisdom in picking those people you can confide in for counsel.

There is a madness behind this story. I was reading in Jonah the other day and thought about this. This is one of my favorite books in the Bible, and it holds many principles of life. In chapter one, it says,

> "One day long ago, God's Word came to Jonah, Amittai's son: 'Up on your feet and on your way to the big city of Nineveh! Preach to them. They're in a bad way and I can't ignore it any longer.' But Jonah got up and went the other direction to Tarshish, running away from God. He went down to the port of Joppa and found a ship headed for Tarshish. He paid the fare and went on board, joining those going to Tarshish—as far away from God as he could get" (MSG).

What if Jonah had a friend whom he trusted and could have asked, "What do you think about this?" Would the outcome have been any different? Would he still have run from God? I'm not sure what I would have said to Jonah; maybe I would have agreed with him and told him to run because the people in Nineveh were crazy. Maybe I would have said, "Let's pray and seek God on this; He will confirm this for you and give you the strength you will need in this task."

The point I am making is in life you can't always go it alone. God has given you friends for a reason; you may need an extra set of eyes and an extra set of ears for any given circumstance. So, give up that old prideful attitude; give up that spirit of embarrassment; and give up that fear of being told something you don't want to hear. Remember, you are asking them for a word of advice, and it's up to you if you want to act on their suggestions. But before you ask anybody for anything, ask God first.

Still Running

I recently turn sixty-two. There is something about getting older that makes you think about your life. Some days, I wake up and hit the ground running, and some days I just seem to crawl. I feel like I've been running for a long time. My life's journey has been an unfiltered and authentic experience.

My run began at five years of age when I was first removed from my home. I soon learned there were others just like me who were running. Even today, there are so many *runners* that I can't count them. I'm not sure if they even know they are running. There's an invisible force we are running against.

It was difficult to identify the runner beside me; for years it directed the course of the life. It controlled every aspect of my speech, my emotions, and my thoughts. Its goal was to cause me to end the run early. This runner, as invisible as it was, had such control of my life. A smile, a hug, or a look could trigger this invisible runner to rise up and fill my mind with evil thoughts.

Through a series of life-changing events in 2005 and 2006, I discovered this runner beside me. In 2007, I came to identify the runner as "the invisible soul." It's a part of every human being's fabric. It's an outside invisible influence that, if given permission, will steer the course of our lives. This runner never runs out of breath and it never sleeps. I'm not talking about the Spirit of God, our spirit, or even our soul. I'm not even talking about the dark spirits of this earth. I am talking about an invisible soul that no one ever sees and is hidden deep in our personality DNA. Of course, there is no scientific study to prove this. The only proof of its existence is the destruction it leaves behind. The death of our innocence and the death of ourselves.

It's what has been introduced to us during our formative years. It seeks no good in our lives as it desires to portray a fake image of who we are to the world, but never our authentic selves. It causes us to run off course from God's plan for our lives. To demystify the invisible soul, it's a dynamic and resonant voice that screams to us to make the choices we make but also whispers ever so softly. The invisible soul wants us to follow and not lead.

The invisible soul has been accelerated into fame by the invention of social media. Its pace is rapid, running alongside countless individuals who may not even be aware of its presence. It runs with those aspiring to be more than what they were created to be. It runs with those who have a double life, one visible and one concealed. It echoes the dynamics of the platforms we navigate today.

Why would anyone let an invisible force be so dominant over their life? The answer is simple but complex at the same time.

How can you run and never know you are running? How can you be in a race but never know there is a race going on? How can something be invisible but identified at the same time? These unseen forces are tangible with the goal of either elevating our sense of achievement or suppressing us so deeply that we decide to end the run early. There is no simple answer to this question. We don't control the invisible soul; it acts on its own accord.

After a two-year journey with an incredible ministry, I was able to come face-to-face with this invisible soul. It wasn't until 2007 that I knew this invisible force existed. I fought hard for these two years as the force was almost too much. The events that took place were seemly directed right at me. Death and destruction were all around me. Then, some thirteen years later, I would confront a force so strong that it almost caused me to end the race. It was as if this invisible soul had laid dormant for years, studying me and observing me, calculating my destruction.

This time was different, though. I had help. For years, I handled things on my own, never seeking help from anyone. It was the way I learned at an early age to deal with myself. In 2007, I believed that unveiling the invisible soul would be the catalyst for its death; that was far from the truth.

My help came from my beautiful wife of forty years. Over the years, I learned to share with Lisa and lean on her; we discovered things together and brought light to what was going on in my inner thoughts. Lisa calls it *checking in with me*.

Through this process of checking in, we discovered I was once again dealing with a force that was not friendly with me. I told Lisa that we had a friend I thought could help to deal with this and put this invisible soul in the grave for the last time. I contacted my now close friend and shared the situation with her, and she agreed to meet with us. She had read my book by then, so the term "the invisible soul" was not a new concept to her. I detailed this encounter in a previous story called "Perspective."

After being in therapy for over two and a half years now, I feel like I am evolving to my purpose and discovering my true path. The run is not so blind; I see now that the path is clear. I have been broken to pieces but put back together with understanding and love. I am more than blessed to have hope in my heart and discover new and exciting truths about myself.

There is a level of hope in my heart that is not measurable. My soul will now live unhindered by an invisible force. I've been lost, but now I am found.

Sometimes I feel guilty for being so free because I know so many who need help. They either refuse or deny the help or they just don't know they need help. It took me years to discover this invisible soul that sought nothing but destruction for me. As the therapist says, "Keep writing; it may help others." Knowing someone has gone before them gives hope to the hopeless and brings love to those who may discover this kind of grace. Love is not deserved but given.

Because it's so, I will live.

Keep running and recognize those who run with you, seen or unseen. This world needs you! Keep running!

in His wakes
"When you pass through the waters, I will be with you" Is. 43:2

An Amazing Journey

As many of you may know, God allowed me to be involved in a water sports ministry for two years in 2005 and 2006. My experiences there helped me to grow in my spiritual walk. Looking back now, I can see right where God had me and why. Many of my stories are accounts of what took place at those events, as they were so life-changing. I am no longer part of that ministry as God has moved me in a new direction. I praise God for the times I had there and love all the people I met. This story originated in Texas. We were working with an extraordinary group of volunteers and a group of kids who were in an emergency shelter. Read my account as it takes you halfway through the season.

The journey this year has been more than amazing. Lots of highs and so many lows. The mountain tops have been high, and the lows have been crushing. Honestly, my life was changed forever in Texas. When I pulled up on the site, I met this kind lady, Terri. I had talked with her many times before via email and phone. She had every detail in order, all the paperwork done, the boats in the water, and volunteers willing to give their entire day for these kids.

I thought to myself, "This is going to be a relaxing day." Terri even asked me, "What do you want to do, just ride in the boat?" "Sure," I replied quickly. I needed a break. We were in the midst of many events, and it was so refreshing to see that they had everything planned out. We had a brief meeting with the volunteers. *What a wonderful group of people,* I thought as I talked. You could tell they were ready to pour out their love to these kids. Skiing was not the focus of the day. It was the kids.

The kids arrived; there were several older teens in the group. So off we went to the boats, allowing most of them to ski. This club really knew what they were doing. At one point, our boat came in, and I got out for a bit. I was just hanging around and talking with the kids. I am always interested in their stories. So, I asked, "What's your story?" Each time I asked this, I got, as expected, the deepest and most devastating accounts of their lives. Not sure why that was, but it just happened that way.

One girl I talked to told me, "All I want to do is go home; I just want to be with my family." Her story can never be repeated as she told it. It was horrific to say the least. It was a true picture of the depravity of man. Not all was hopeless, though. She still had dreams and shared a few of them with me. One thing that I noticed was her eyes. As I looked past her pretty, green eyes, I could see the pain I had seen all summer long. It's in the eyes. I tried not to look, but they kept drawing me in. *Please help me*, they cried out. I remember praying for her in my heart right where I was standing. After talking to her, I just shook my head in disbelief. I was hurting.

At the end of every event, I was able to talk with the kids about life and God's love for them. As I was talking to this group of kids under the tent that day, I looked over to my right, and there she was, standing almost up front with me, just staring at me. I don't think I will ever forget those eyes as I shared the message of the Gospel that day, a message of hope that I knew could change her life. Something was missing, and I knew what it was. It was the love of Christ in her heart. At the end of the day, all of the kids left and took most of their pain with them. I say most of their pain because I took some of it with me.

To remember that year, I reflect on that little girl's eyes. I learned through this to give less of me and more of the Gospel, more of God's word, and more of the Love of Christ. This is the true message of hope, not my life experiences, but the life of Christ.

As I gave the invitation, I raised my head, opened my eyes, and I saw those beautiful eyes. I could hear the cries from deep in her soul, and I could feel the pain she had been through. I was not giving up. "Will you come? Will you come?" I cried. All the while knowing *I* could do nothing. It is all God who gives this hope of life, not me. I wanted to go over and put my arm around her and tell her how much Jesus loved her, but I knew God would speak to her heart. She looked up at me, and our eyes locked again. I told her Jesus loved her and that He could help her deal with all that she was carrying. All I could do was thank God for all He had done.

Over the past two days, we have seen more people come to Christ than ever before. I was asked, "Why do you think that is"? I have so many things going on in my heart right now, so all I can say is less of me and more of God. The power is in the Gospel; the power is in God's word and not mine. I am dying to myself.

That is where I am at right now. Dying to myself. As I spend more time in those crushing moments, I am learning to deny self and depend on God in every moment. I am also convinced that the human eyes and mind can only take in so much. As I sit here in this airport, I am in tears, reflecting on the last two weeks. Unable to talk about it any longer, but just hoping to write and get it out of my mind.

I am close to collapse as my mind and soul can only take so much of living in a world that is all too familiar to me. The pain and the suffering I take in, not knowing what to do with it. Where can I pass it on? Who can I pass it on to? Will you take it, Lord? Please help me!

To My Mom

As I sit here and ponder on this story, the emotions needed to explore this may be too much. I'm just not sure; the door is *yellow*, which means enter, but be cautious in this journey. As you know, *red doors* are the only ones off limits right now for me.

I'm still sitting here, thinking about where to start. This story is much more difficult than the last. It seems there is a stop sign ahead, and I'm going to pay attention to it. I'm going to stop; it looks like an all way stop. I'm looking in all directions and seeing lots of thoughts and emotions at all the stop signs, a traffic jam of emotions. I want and need to write this out. A trusted member of my community has encouraged me to take it slowly and just let the story develop. I need to examine how each of these thoughts and emotions speaks to me. This is a more natural therapeutic process. Thank you, trusted friend.

The last story took so much out of me, but I want to press forward. I have waved these emotions on in different directions, and we will see them deeper in the story. I think they were just warning me of what was to come, and I'm okay with that. The door is still cracked, and I can escape if I need to. Always have an escape plan.

So, I'm sitting here at this all way stop, and I've been courteous and waved all the *thoughts and emotions* on. I'm the only one left here at the stop sign, and it's my turn to go. So here we go, "To My Mom."

It's been two weeks now, and I realize why I haven't written any words down. I spotted a red door emotion at one of those stop signs. It has been in the forefront of my mind since waving all those emotions and thoughts through. Those thoughts and emotions are very real and a part of this story, but not right now.

I got out of my car at the all way stop and walked right up to the car window, just like I did when I was eighteen years old. I punched out all the windows in the car, including the back glass and the windshield and told him to leave and never come back. I threw everything he had in the yard and never saw him again. That evil man had one goal for me and that was death. I guess he finally saw the evil in my eyes. If he had spoken one word to me that day, I would be in prison today.

That's the thing most abusers don't get; we all grow up. At some point, we will be able to defend ourselves. He thought the torture he inflected on me would have been enough for me to submit to his every word. But not that day! I hope you can feel and sense the (powerful) emotions expressed here.

It has to stay away right now.

That's one of the beautiful things of discovering and exploring these emotions; they are complex and so many are woven together. No matter the door you label them in, they have a way of making it to the front of our thoughts and can even rule our emotions. So, with that said, we are moving forward with this story. "To My Mom."

To My Mom: Sometimes, I can't understand why. Why did you decide to have me if you knew you couldn't care for me? Why would you have me if you knew? Maybe you just had a dream of a family full of love, peace, and happiness. The dream trumped all rationale.

To My Mom: Your choices in men were the worst. You picked the ones who hated me. You picked the ones who wanted nothing but death for me. Even my own dad killed himself. So, death seems to be the curse that has followed me on this journey of life. You chose four people to be a father to me and none were more than ashes to me.

To My Mom: I look at the few pictures that I have of me when I was a child. I must admit, they make me smile and warm my heart. I can think there was a time that it may have been okay. There may have been a time that I was loved, hugged, and taken care of. The latter part of my childhood seems to erase all of that. It's like going from a beautiful sunny day to an all-out deep, dark storm.

To My Mom: Some say, "beauty comes from pain." Some say, "beauty comes out of the ashes when you walk through a fire." I get this, Mom. It is true. If we all had perfect childhoods, then who helps those who don't? Who can direct them to the right places to get the help they need?

To My Mom: Our relationship never developed until the last two weeks of your life. I spent every night in the hospital with you watching you die. The cancer had finally won. You just wanted to know I was there, and I was. I felt like I loved you the way you loved me when I was just two weeks old. The love that is unconditional and has no borders. It was difficult watching you die, and my heart aches every day not to have your presence on this earth, as you were my mom.

To My Mom: When I look at pictures of you now, you are but a memory, just like we all will be one day. A picture on a wall for a few years at least, and then we are forgotten. In years to come, our plight is unknown to those who come behind us. Mom, all I can hope is someday someone will be browsing and stumble upon this story. I hope they read it, and it encourages them; I hope they can see that beauty comes from pain and hope rises.

To My Mom: I truly love you! I forgive you! I'm asking myself if that is enough. I'm approaching that all way stop, and the thoughts and emotions that have stopped here have moved on. I believe that's what love and forgiveness bring, a life full of flowing happiness, a life that is beautiful. Thank you, Mom, for being there and for doing the best you could do. It had to be scary and heartbreaking at the same time. I'm not mad. I'm not angry. I am loved.

I know through writing this story that you love me, and I believe you forgave me for not being the best son I could have been. Even in the best times, I was not so good. You know in your heart as a mom that I was doing my best. I love you, Mom. I miss you!

To My Mom: Beauty from pain, broken to life, beauty from ashes, amazing grace. Yes! You gave that to me. I love you.

MATTHEW S BEASLEY JR
NORTH CAROLINA
SGT US MARINE CORPS
WORLD WAR II KOREA
NOV 17 1926 JAN 6 1974

To My Dad

This is a continuation of my "to my" stories. This one may be abstract because I can't see the person I'm talking about; I can't see him as a daddy at all. I can't see him as a man whom I was born after; I can't even see him as a person. Memories are the foundational development of who we are as humans. This story has come to me after more than two years, visiting a wonderful therapist.

If you read some of my backstories, you will see that I have been constantly growing into who I am at age sixty-one. Who would have thought? Some have asked me why I go to therapy. Why don't you just let it go? Why put yourself through this? What is your end goal here? My answer is simple; I want freedom, and I want peace in every area of my life. Each story I write releases a part of me that has been in chains for years. I have to release these stories.

I want to leave a legacy in words for those who will come after me. I want those who have fallen to my plight to be encouraged that there is hope. You can live a life full of peace and happiness and a life full of love. It is possible to not know where you came from, but to know there is hope. There is love that is born out of not knowing who loved you first. So with that, here it goes, "to my dad."

To My Dad: I knew you but never knew you! You never gave me a chance to know you. You left me too soon. Before I could understand who you were, you left me. You left me! I am feeling anger and sadness in writing this.

To My Dad: What hurts me the most is I don't remember ever saying the word, "daddy." That may have been the very first word out of my mouth. The first word I learned may have been "daddy." I'm just not sure. I have no memory of those early years.

To My Dad: I needed a protector later in my childhood, and you were already gone. I was being tortured, and you were nowhere to be found. Where were you? I needed you so much, but you were never there. I was beaten and left for dead more than once; I needed you! Why did you leave me?

To My Dad: When I cried, you were not there to comfort me. I was in tears, and you were already gone. You never saw me cry, never saw my tears, never heard my voice of helplessness. In the darkness, I needed my daddy, but you were gone. I can't say you didn't care, but you just couldn't give what I needed. All I needed was to be loved. That's all I ever wanted.

To My Dad: You never saw me play ball at the park; you never saw me off to school; you never met my teachers; and you never helped me with my homework. I know you had something that you could have imparted to me, but I missed all of that because you left too soon.

To My Dad: You would have been a great granddaddy! My grandchildren would have loved to have known you, but they don't even know your name. They never ask who their great granddaddy is. This is so sad, and it makes me cry when I think about it. They would have loved your presence and your love that you could have shared with them.

To My Dad: I hope that at some point in your life you called on the God of hope to help you through the struggles you were having. Now I know they were so heavy on you that life itself escaped you. The struggle ultimately took your life and part of mine as well.

To My Dad: I never got a hug from you; I never got a kiss from you; I never got a "I love you" from you. I think that's why it made me want to love my girls even more. I missed all of this because you decided it was just too much for you. It seems selfish, but I wasn't in your struggle as an active player.

To My Dad: I needed rescuing, and you were already gone. What was I to do and feel beside your casket at the age of twelve? They had already removed me at age five, in and out of this torturous life. Seven years had gone by, and I cried every night since you left me with this evil step. I dare don't call him father as he had no father qualities. This man was so evil and wanted nothing but death for me and my siblings. The system was and is broken, as it put me in and out of human danger until I was old enough to protect myself.

To My Dad: I will never be sure why, but one thing is certain, you gave me life, and for that I am thankful. It has not been an easy road, but it has been a road none the less. I am thankful that at some point you actually loved my mom. I am thankful that at some point you may have said, "I love you," and kissed me. I am thankful that God placed you on this planet to have a part in my life. I am thankful that you may have cared for me at some point in my life. You may not have been the best father, but you are still my father. Today If I could speak to you, I would tell you I love you and forgive you.

To My Dad: I can see now that there was so much on you that you felt you had no choice but to end it all. That seems to follow me in my life, but I'm determined not to follow you, as I love this life way too much. There is so much more to give. I want to bring hope, joy, and love to my grandchildren, my daughters, my son-in-loves, and my wonderful love of over forty years now, my sweet Lisa.

To My Dad: So, when I visit your grave these days, I just say, "thank you." Thank you for creating me; thank you for the part you played in my life. Thank you with tears. I miss you, Daddy, and I truly love you!

The Shooter

(I wrote this in memory of my dad)

Why did he pull the trigger that day,
Leaving me this way?

I'm still so sad after all these years.
So many tears, so many years.

I often wonder which way did he die?
From the front or from the side?

The voices were loud I know.
Why?

Was it Mother or me?
Brothers and sisters have suffered so much.
The pain goes deep, and the voices are loud.

Daddy, why did you go?
Daddy, I didn't know.

Why did you go?

The pain before the shot must have been loud.
The pain after the shot still rings now.

Why?
Couldn't you see,
There was so much to me?

I think of you as you stared into my big brown eyes,
Gave me a kiss,
And said goodbye.

I love you so much, even today.
I blamed myself, as it helped the pain.
But figured out that's not the way.

Daddy, the only thing I can say,
You would be so proud of me this way.

I love you so much, even today.

I Love You!

Through my journey to open emotional doors locked away for many years, I have stumbled on a host of lost and forgotten doors.

It's the holiday season, and I wanted to write about a season of love that took place in the summer of 2005. It's not a love like you are thinking about but a new love that I was shown. Love is not something you say but something you do. That's the whole point of this story.

Now would be a good time to explain the doors of emotions that have evolved over the past few years. They are all labeled in my mind. Some are locked, some are doubled locked, and each door is painted a color, green, yellow, and red. You have guessed it right; green is go, open, and explore; yellow is cautiously go but be ready to back out if needed; and red is no, not now, do not enter. I can walk by each door visually in my mind and my soul, spirit, and human emotion can let me know how to explore each of these safely.

The door we are cracking today has a backstory that is totally red, but the front story is green, so I feel safe in opening this very positive door. It's the point and time I learned to say to another human, "I love you!"

I've always told my wife, my girls, and some family members that I love them, and I meant it; I truly loved them. Something happened in the summer of 2005 that would change me and prepare me for the next event that is behind a red door that happened in the summer of 2006. That door is labeled, "Silence, Do Not Enter!" Just writing this makes me want to explore that door, but I know I'm not ready even after seventeen years have passed. So, I'm going to stay on track with this open green door, which is life changing for me. It has been screaming at me for weeks now to say it's time to write, "I love you."

I woke up this morning at about 2:30 am, and the story was coming together. In 2005, I traveled to St. Louis to meet up with a team of people who were changing America. I remember walking into the office and asking to speak with my contact, Pastor Jami. She greeted me at the door, and we sat and talked for what seemed like hours. We discussed joining together to meet the needs of the lost and forgotten people of this world. My mission was to bring people hope, comfort, and peace and to bring them to a knowledge of Jesus and His wonderful grace. I then got to meet with her husband, Pastor Jeff. We sat and talked even more. I left with the hope that we could work together in the future.

I'm not really sure how it came to be, but I got a phone call from Jami, and she said she thought we could work together for a ministry event in the summer of 2005. I was so excited about this. This story is not about the event that would soon take place but about the people involved with the event.

It's not relevant what the ministry was but that we changed the lives of those we ministered to in a unique way. We can call it *bringing Jesus to the water with love*. This is safe for me, staying away from that red door we just mentioned.

I flew back to St Louis to plan for the event, and I had checked into the motel. Jami called to tell me they would pick me up from the motel, and she invited me to stay with them for the duration of my trip. I was resistant, as I really didn't know them that well, but it seemed like I had known them for years. I arrived at their mountaintop house and was treated like the rest of the family. I felt the love just pouring out of them. Jeff asked if I liked steak, and of course, I said, "Yes." He said that we were going to make some fantastic ones. He salted the steaks, and it looked like it snowed on top of them. They led me to the room I would be staying in for the next few days. This home was so beautiful. They were a family of love and compassion, and hope just poured out of them. That's what I remember the most.

The steaks were delicious, and the meal was outstanding. Jami said, "Get ready, because *Lost* is coming on, and we don't want to miss that." So, we all went downstairs and sat on the couch and comfy chairs and watched *Lost*. I had never seen it, but I was instantly a fan.

The next day, I explored the inner city with their ministry. The goal for that day was if you see a need then do everything in your power to meet that need. Whatever it was, meet the need. I had never seen anything like that, ever.

Jeff and I were walking near his office and gunshots rang out. I asked if we were okay, and he assured me we were safe. This is the start of my experience of what love is and how it would change me.

Later that evening, people were milling around the campus for a ministry event. A very nice man walked up to Jeff and asked him for money. Jeff's reply changed me forever. He said, "Silver and gold I do not have, but I have the love of Christ. Would you like that instead?"

The man replied, "Yes, of course!" He then looked at me and said, "George, share Jesus with this man." It sounds like a story from the Bible, but I promise you I said, "Would you like to know Jesus as your savior?" And he said, "Yes." So, I led him to Jesus.

This is how it was with Jeff and Jami. They seemed to bring love with them wherever they went. I was blessed to hear Jeff preach a powerful message on the power of the Holy Spirit that evening. I even went up front and grabbed some anointing oil, which I still have today, and it never seems to run out. I have used it often in tough times and in times of need.

I would be remiss to leave out the most important part of my journey. We returned to their home that evening, and I got on my knees to pray in my room. It wasn't long into my prayer that the robe of Jesus passed right by my eyes, and I met the Holy Spirit of God in that place. I met the Spirit in a way that truly changed me forever. Love had a new meaning, but I wasn't sure what was happening in that moment. It was well with my soul.

Later that week, I visited another ministry and heard Jeff give his personal testimony of how God saved him from a life of drugs and a life of destruction. I could not believe my ears. God is truly greater than I could ever imagine. I felt like I was walking around with Paul of the Bible. During one of our conversations, Jeff told me I had put God in a tiny box. "He is much bigger than that, George," he said. I totally agreed!

It was time for me to go home, and they took me to the airport to drop me off. We sat out in the parking lot of the airport, and they wanted to pray with me. I leaned forward from the back seat, and they laid hands on my head and started praying for me. This was all new to me; I felt something so new, so full of love, and so beautiful. After the prayer, we got out of the car, and it happened. Jeff grabbed my shoulders, looked me in the eyes, and said, "I love you, friend." Then Jami came around from the left, went under my arm, and gave me the biggest hug ever and said, "I love you!" I must say, I felt a bit uneasy. Telling people I loved them seemed strange to me.

On the long plane ride home, I had the urge to tell people I met and made eye contact with that I loved them. Thanks to Jeff and Jami, I learned that I loved them, and I loved people, regardless of their position in life. Love trumps all things. That's what they taught me, along with the Holy Spirt of God, to love all people. All I have to give is the Love of Christ.

Seventeen years ago, I met some amazing people who taught me to love humans without a lens and without a filter. This season, don't judge, love. Love unconditionally; love where the spirit leads you; love where your faith leads you; and love deeper than you ever have. Love is not something you just say, but something you do.

To My Girls

I love you!

So, with that said, that could be the end of the story. The truth is, though, my love for my girls is only the beginning. For the past few stories, I have focused on the memories and emotions that come along with all that. It's been happy and sad all at the same time. I have been able to navigate these new waters at my age with the help and guidance of some unique people in my community.

A good friend came by recently and we talked about a story I am writing in parallel with this one; she encouraged me to focus on the one that is most pressing in my mind. She told me she was happy that we were a part of her community. Life is about community if you think about it. That's another story.

This story has been brewing in my mind for several months now and it's finally time to escape the boundaries of my mind and enter my thoughts into words.

I remember when my sweet Lisa told me she was pregnant with our first girl. I was scared to death, thinking, what are we in for here? How can I raise a girl in this world? I need guns and bullets! Then, a year and a half later, we had another girl! Oh, Lord! What was I to do? We were just barely making it financially, working three jobs most of the time, but loving every minute.

Providing for my family was ingrained in my being. Being removed at age five, I was determined not to repeat history. My girls would see a life that was full of love and joy. Not necessarily things, but just love and joy; knowing they were loved was the most important.

To be quite honest, I have been running from these emotions that are brewing in my soul for months now; just the thought of writing this has become so difficult. I wake up every morning with thoughts of finishing this story, but something always comes up that prevents me from engaging in it. I'm now in week eight, and I've only written a few words here and there. That explains all the rambling in the front end of this story.

With everything in me, I love my girls! We have been blessed to have a wonderful relationship and a bond that is like no other. *To My Girls* was born out of the last two stories, and I don't want them to read this story until I am no longer on this earth. I'm sure that won't be the case.

I love you girls. All I ever wanted was for you to be loved and for you both to live a beautiful life, full of joy, happiness, and love. I believe God has blessed me with that for the most part. My beautiful, sweet Lisa (my wife) has endured so much in this life and is worthy of such a blessing of peace and harmony. I've asked God so many times to take whatever blessing He has had for me and give it to you and my girls. I don't truly understand what love means, but given life or death, I would take the place of my girls if I could. So, here we go.

Girls, I want you to know that my heart has been so full over the years; raising you both was the most amazing and beautiful event in my life. Nothing compares to that.

Lisa, you know I have done everything possible to mess this up, but you have fought for us, and for that I am so full of the newness of your love every single day.

Girls, I want you to know that the joy and love you have brought me has extended the days of my life; you have been instrumental in the healing process of my mind and soul.

Lisa, the love you have rained down on me has brought me great strength and focus to be the best I can be. Your love has forged a straight path that has given me hope and a promise of tomorrow.

Girls, your existence has brought me overwhelming love, feelings of pain, and feelings of great joy. All I ever wanted was to show you love and teach you how to love, and I believe I have done that. No matter how far from the shore I went, I could always see you; I could always feel you and experience your pain and joy.

Lisa, we have experienced so much over the past forty years. In the midst of intense attacks and extraordinary togetherness, love has prevailed. We have been desperate at times, and we have been on the mountaintops at times. Through it all, we came through that season. Sometimes we had to dust off the ashes, and sometimes we came out looking brand new. That has always made us who we were, ready for the next season. The storms and the beautiful calmness of the water have taught us to trust.

Girls, you are now grown, and I can only hope that I have given you all you will need to make it through each and every season in life—the good, the bad, the ugly, and the beautiful. I pray that this life is more kind to you than it has been to me. Life may not be fair at times, but always keep hope in front of your eyes. I hope that you see the good in all people, and understand that everyone needs a smile, a hug, a kiss, and just a kind word. I love you girls with all my heart and soul. This love I can't explain.

Lisa, I have gained this tremendous knowledge over the past two years that love has no boundaries, and that when our love is expressed, it can overcome all things and climb insurmountable mountains. You have sat so patiently with me for so many hours as I discovered these new truths and the emotions that I have kept hidden for so many years.

Girls, what I will miss the most is your kisses and the beautiful hugs you give me every time we see each other. I will miss the dinners we shared, the laughter we shared, and the cries we shared. I will miss the looks you give your children, and the instruction you give them minute-by-minute. I will miss your husbands and the conversations we have had over the years. I will miss you getting old and experiencing this beautiful change in life. I will miss my grandchildren and seeing the wonderful impact they will have on humanity. I will miss their beautiful hugs. I will miss being loved by you.

Lisa, with everything, I will miss your beautiful awaking each day; looking at you as I wake up every day has been a wonderful blessing. I will miss the sun shining on your lovely face and the calmness and tranquility you have brought to my soul. I will miss the sunrises and the sunsets we have shared together. I will miss the boat rides, the ski rides, the conversations about life, and the conversations about the life to come. We have traveled an extraordinary journey together. There has to be a word larger than love that can describe the emotions I am feeling; the tears that are streaming down my face right now are soaking my shirt as I write this. I will say, I love you!

So, now that you are reading this, I may or may not be here on this earth. I've worked hard to keep this story hidden in a safe place. By now, I've already told you all this, anyway. There is something about words that live forever and that is the point of this story. I want you, my girls, and my sweet Lisa, to go back and see my words and experience them over and over. When you get lonely or sad, or just need a word of encouragement, come here. You will now be able to see that I cracked the door to the emotions I kept inside of my soul, deeper that even I knew existed. You are my girls and I'm thankful and blessed. I have surrendered everything that I am to your love and to your beautiful grace. I love you!

CORAL

Emotions

Emotions are extremely powerful. I have avoided them my whole life. I didn't cry; I didn't look sad, ever. All I ever did was smile. A fake facade to so many for so many years.

So why am I writing about these emotions today? For the last twenty-four months, I have been given permission to engage these emotions in a way I never thought possible. As I exited my therapy session last week, my therapist encouraged me to engage those emotions, good or bad, and experience the joy or pain of what was to come. I wasn't sure if I could do it. I wasn't sure if I was ready for this experience, this life of genuine emotions. I had hidden for so many years from these "feelings."

As the therapist spoke to me, I wondered if she thought I was ready for this. She had concerns herself but thought I should take the time and effort to explore my feelings.

What was my escape plan if it went wrong? Shut down! Run! Just walk away if I need to; I always have an escape plan.

We invited our daughter, son-in-law, and their two sons down to the lake house for the weekend. I decided to be fully engaged in whatever activity was going on; that included experiencing emotions that might be uncomfortable or even joyous. At first, I enjoyed the surface play and joy of being with my grandchildren; it was an experience that I had been avoiding for the last eight years. My grandsons are now five and seven years old. I didn't realize it had been that many years until just now.

We played in the water for most of the day, just us and them, no big deal. There was no emotional detail to speak of, and then, like the flip of a switch, it happened.

The sun shone just right on the five-year-old, causing a glow around his tiny body as he stood on the dock. With wet footprints on the dock from his path out of the water, he took off, running down the dock to jump in the lake, screaming loudly with excitement. He surfaced with joy, laughter, and complete happiness.

I was fully engaged, emotionally. This seemed dangerous and somewhat scary. As I gazed at him in the sunlight, I thought, *he is who I was but even more blessed than me.*

I was removed from my family at his age. I was completely separated from the most dangerous, violent, torturous environment that a child of five-years-old should have ever encountered.

I watched him as I went back in time and realized that tears were streaming down my face; my heart was hurting so badly. I was experiencing this for the first time because I had given myself permission to engage these emotions.

I wondered what kind of mom would allow her five-year-old to be removed from the family? Then, it hit me. My mom saw there was no hope for me there in that environment. No hope, only death, and beating after beating, torture after torture, kick after kick, lack after lack, and nothing but destruction on the horizons; she was a good mom. Really, can I say that now? Yes!

We harbor so many emotions that make us who we are. Sometimes, we need permission to explore these emotions and see what they may uncover to help develop us into what we are destined to become. We are complex, loving, emotional, happy, sad, and beautiful people.

As I watched my grandson, it was like watching who I could have been. He is so blessed to be living his best life and not having to worry about being beaten, tortured, hungry, or homeless. He is free to be only who he is, loved and happy. He is experiencing life at a level I never knew. I am grateful to God to know that the chains have been broken, that the enemy is defeated, and that evil didn't prevail.

In the end, I found out it was okay to explore these emotions and new fears that pop up because of this exploration. Give yourself permission, take it slowly, and relax when you need to. Learn when to stay and when to walk away; also, it's okay to say no. It's okay to be who you are, and those around you who know your struggle will understand and be kind. Some will understand and some will judge because they cannot empathize and understand your struggles.

Writing this and other stories has helped me discover a hidden chest of emotions and experiences I have been suppressing for many years. Note, I didn't say treasure chest because I'm not sure if they are treasures just yet. Some have left me in tears and caused me deep sadness. However, writing about these stories has given me great freedom in my soul. I hope that releasing these emotions will bring healing that seemed impossible just two years ago.

It's so easy to ignore our feelings and not deal with difficult emotions that may take us to unpleasant places in our lives. But it's important to take the steps to open up. Then healing can bring positive changes that foster love and authentic relationships, true healing, and a more meaningful life.

Perspective

At almost sixty years of age, I thought I would be experiencing peace, joy, happiness, love and all the other exceptional things life has to offer. I have experienced these things in the past. However, over the past two years, terror has invaded my soul and my mind and has brought me many sleepless nights and thoughts of death. Trauma from early childhood abuse has resurfaced with a vengeance and is desperate to take over my mind and put my soul to rest for good.

The memories are so intrusive that they materialize at any moment; the pain is real, and the experiences are like fresh wounds. I can feel the emotional pain and the hits; my head jars and my body moves with motions of the torture. It was more than a hit to the head or gut and getting up off the floor just to be there again. Sometimes I would lay on the floor and act as if I couldn't stand up; that would often come with a kick to the head or stomach, but it wasn't worth it to be knocked down again. Seeing those legs and shoes turn in a different direction and walk away was a relief. I would tell myself, "It's over for now."

So, why am I sharing this with you? Writing about my past brings my memories to life and out in the open; they have been in hiding for so many years. I've referred to my past as an "invisible soul." Trauma can drive you and kill you if you let it take over. I know it sounds a bit psychotic, but the reality is your memories can kill you. I know so many people who have let their past destroy them. I've been thinking a great deal about them lately.

I had a nightmare a few weeks ago that I sat on the end of the bed with a gun in my hand. I found it hard not to pull the trigger. It was so real; I was out of my body, watching the event unfold. I could see myself walking toward the gun and then holding the gun in my hand. I stared at it and wondered what it was. Was my life about to end? After waking up, I was asking myself, "Was that real?" I even looked for the gun to make sure I hadn't moved it. Thankfully, I hadn't. My sweet Lisa has since moved the gun.

As the flashbacks and thoughts of harming myself got worse, I sought help! I just happened to have a friend who is a wonderful therapist. She agreed to see me, and Lisa went along with me; after thirty-seven years of marriage, we are in this together! I had shared my struggles with Lisa before seeking help. She was in agreement that we needed to meet with a therapist.

The first session was not weird at all because I knew my therapist and had often joked with her that I was in need of a "session." We sat down and her first question was, "When was the last time you were in therapy?" She already knew some of my story but not to the depths that she would soon learn. I told her it had been more than forty years since my last session. At that point, I shared with her the trauma I had been facing lately. I told her, "It seems that I'm not getting through this, and I'm not sure if I will." "Tell me more about what's going on, George," she said. These words echoed in my soul as I had not heard that question in more than forty years.

After a few sessions, I began to put things back into perspective. Don't get me wrong, I'm not there yet, and I'm not sure if I will get "there." But what I do know is that I have to identify what triggers these memories/flashbacks and how they create specific emotions. It is not an easy task.

It requires me to look at each memory, understand why it's being presented to my mind at that time, and try and expose what caused it to surface.

The dreams were lifelike to give my mind the perspective of what that event would look like if it played out. It was quite a relief to know that my thoughts and dreams were not abnormal. My triggers could be a place, smell, person, certain walk, specific day, funeral, sound, song, or food. On a side note, the therapist did expose that I didn't have a plan to carry out my suggestive murder, and that is a good thing!

For now, this is the plan of exposing and managing these memories. We have identified that my mental health is tied directly to my level of exhaustion. When I am tired, stressed, overwhelmed, or feel out of control, I start to regress back to an unhealthy state of mind. This knowledge has helped me tremendously. So, the plan right now is to keep identifying the trauma and not take on more than I can handle. Triggers are important, and I believe we all have them—some worse than others.

As of late, I have more joy and peace and have been enjoying my life. If you find yourself experiencing disturbing thoughts and dreams from past traumas, please seek help. Sometimes it takes a good friend, an experienced therapist, and a wonderful wife to help put things into perspective.

Haven House

Isaiah 49:10-11 (MSG) says, "Nobody hungry, nobody thirsty, shade from the sun, shelter from the wind, For the Compassionate One guides them, takes them to the best springs. I'll make all my mountains into roads, turn them into a superhighway."

Let me bring you to a time in my early teen years. Haven House was my second group home. It was to be short-term. I had a great deal of people who cared about me, but my stubborn attitude pushed many away. Although young, I learned so many life lessons there. This was a time before the *mental games* were introduced into troubled teens' lives. I call them mental games because, as time went forward, we all learned how to beat the system. The system being ideas like *if you let them think this, then they will act this way*. Haven House was not that way at all; they taught us by life itself, teaching us that for every action, negative or positive, there would be a reaction and a price to pay at some level. I hope you immerse yourself in this story as it is as true as it gets. Lord willing, I will take you from this point in my life to the present day in the upcoming stories. Here is the Haven House story as I saw it and remember it today.

There was much controversy in the neighborhood on Shepard Street. This thing called a home for troubled youth was coming. Maybe now, looking back, we were pioneers of our present-day culture, and Haven House was the pioneering concept of *fixing* us. I already believed that none of the neighbors wanted us there, but that was not new to me. For most of my life, I felt like I was just in the way. The experiences I had there would forever change me, molding me into the person I am today. It was not the experiences that made the difference, but the people.

What influence did the people have on my life? I have an overwhelming, deep desire to tell you that these people who gave their lives to try and teach me something had such a life-changing impact that it would be hard to put into words. I guess what I am saying is that it was never about the experiences but the people. After some thirty years, I can tell you of only a couple of experiences I had, but I can see in my mind and tell you each person's name and what I remember them doing for me.

There was Charlie. I'm not sure what his job was, but I remember him spending time talking to me; that's all we really wanted, to talk and for someone to listen. I remember Anita, who did the same, always with a sweet smile and a warm hello; her eyes would warm your heart no matter how bad things were. She would always ask on a hot summer day, "Would you like something to drink?" Although not part of the Haven House, my court-appointed officer, Ellen, is a part of my memory there. She had an impact that is still lasting on me. I can remember sitting with her and talking things out. She had me do some crazy things with my fingers to test my concentration. I still do that today.

Then there were three: Michael, Peter, and Barbara. They were our house parents. I could go into detail about each one, as they each had their own special way of trying to get into my brain. They, without doubt, are the most interesting people I have ever met. I have so many wonderful memories and could write a book on my experiences with each of them, but to keep this short, I will give you a summary of each one and the impact they had.

We can start with Michael, who loved to meditate; this was his way of teaching us to relax and get in touch with our inner being, if you will. We would sit for hours, sometimes talk, but mostly sit. This was relaxing and taught me a great deal about myself.

Peter loved to write; I am not sure if that is where I developed the love for writing or not. Only to say that he had this big book, and he would sit and write all of what he saw going on. Peter had a kind heart and really loved us. As a matter of fact, all three of these shared the same heart. They truly loved us no matter what. They each represented how God loves us. Peter also loved to cook and grow his own food; thinking back, they all three loved to grow their own food. This is where we would spend time when we did things we were not supposed to do—in *the garden*.

Then there was Barbara. She wore this long robe, sandals, and smoked a pipe. For some reason, I can hear her say, "George, what are your feelings on this?" She was always caring and seemed to be sensitive to feelings. What I remember the most about her is that she loved us.

That was a snapshot of Haven House, from its inception. Keep in mind, this was 1974, and the culture as we know it today was forever changed by the people of Haven House. It was never about the program, the events, or all of the other experiences. It will always be about the people. They showed us they loved us. That is all we ever wanted—to be loved. It's love that makes the difference.

Shoelaces

As I sit here contemplating which of my fifty stories I need to finish, I realize none of them may ever be brought to life. The year 2020 silenced both my time and creativity. I guess you could say I got caught up in the politics and social media events that 2020 presented to us.

I'm acknowledging this as I sit peacefully on my front porch, facing the most beautiful lake in the world. I'm pondering what to write. It's so quiet this time of year, and the raindrops are hitting the ground slowly and making fun in the water. The wind is nowhere to be found, and the temperature is close to sixty-five degrees—mind you, this is January 2021.

Peace instills my soul, and a story is developing in my mind about learning to tie my shoes. What is this story that looms in the distant fog that covers the lake? It's a simple story but applicable to us all.

Let's unpack this from my thought barn. At some point, someone had to teach us how to tie our shoelaces. I have a faint memory of someone teaching me how to tie mine.

There was a repeated step-by-step process instructing me how to tie a complicated knot to keep my shoes firmly in place on the soles of my feet. Each day I would say, "Can you help me tie my shoes?" Each day I would hear the same response, "I will be right there." Then an individual would enter my room, bend down in front of me, and go through the same process as the previous day. Cross the laces, make a bow, then make another bow, circle the lace, and then pull tight.

Day after day, I received the same directions, but I never fully understood the process. The instructions were clear, but my brain could not grasp the simple technique. Then one day when I called for help, a lady came in, sat behind me, and reached her arms around me as to give me a big hug. She grabbed my hands and my shoelaces and said, "Cross the laces, make a bow, then make another bow, wrap, and then pull tight." There it was, as plain as day; I tied my shoes. I never had to ask for help again.

There is something fascinating about the way we are taught and how our brain sees things. As I mentioned early on, 2020 was a year to remember. I don't believe it matters to what extent we learned things. We all grew in some way. Fact or fiction, the stories kept coming last year.

Learning from the Spirit of God is about Him reaching around to embrace me, teaching me His way of doing things, and showing me it's going to be okay. It's not what's in front of me but who has me in His arms. So, for 2021, lean more into God's arms, trust His hugs and His Word, not what's in front of you (e.g., television, social media, friends, or even family).

The Imperfect Move

To an outsider, our lives seem so perfect. We love the idea of creating the perfect life. Our lives are perfect, right?

The norm in our social culture is to appear perfect in front of our peers. We want to be at the top and to be better than any of our friends and family.

I was helping some friends move recently, and when we were ready to load the big stuff, we realized their couch had not been moved in years. It was a rather large leather couch and was more than eight-feet-long. So far in this move, everything seemed perfect—the clothes, toys, and tables were all like new and clean. All this seemed to be indicative of how their lives seemed—perfect.

We had to pull the bottom cushions off the couch to make it lighter and more manageable, and we had to turn it over to get it out the door.

Turns out, the perfect family, the perfect house, and the perfect life had some hidden issues. As we peeled off the couch cushions, there was so much trash and dirt that the homeowner quickly grabbed a handheld vacuum and proceeded to clean this dirt and trash from the couch. I was stunned that this was taking place right before our eyes. This seemingly flawless family was cleaning their dirt right in front of me, as if I didn't see them.

To be honest with you, I knew this family was like that, a portrait of perfection as I call them. If you were to see them you would think, "perfection." If you look at their social media pages, they speak volumes of perfection; they would tell you they are living the ideal life and have nothing but perfect children, perfect clothes, perfect cars, and perfect stuff. They are the best. A perfect family with no dirt and no trash!

I discovered years ago we all have dirt and trash under our cushions. Go to any house in the world, and you will find dirt, old stuff, and trash under their couch cushions.

We all do! So, why do we try to hide our imperfections? Why hasn't this beautiful family figured this out?

Could it be that striving to be perfect has blinded them to their real state of being—imperfection? Blinded by the pursuit of perfection.

I believe striving to portray our lives as perfect only leads us to lift our cushions and look at what a mess we really are. We are a mess, and it's only by God's grace we are made righteous as followers of Jesus. Followers who are okay with our messes and comfortable with our dirt.

May we strive to be followers who acknowledge that our mess is our message and never needs to be hidden under a couch cushion. So, the next time you are helping friends move, look under their couch cushions, and then look at the people. Does their life match their dirt?

God, Are You There?

"Hey, Mike, you there?" I whispered.

"Yes, George," the small voice always answered. "I'm here." I can't tell you how much comfort and peace his voice and words brought me in a time of great trouble.

Being locked in a closet for what seemed like days was normal for me and my brother, Mike. Each day, my mother would drop us off at daycare. After she left, the daycare person would smile at us and immediately tell us to get into that closet.

It was so dark and lonely in there. I would proceed to my corner, pull my knees in tight to my chest, and lay my head onto my legs. My brother would go to the other side of the closet and sit there with his legs crossed. I could see him right before the door closed, right before the darkness set in.

Each day, I would ask that same question. "Mike, are you there?" And he would always respond in his reassuring voice. "Yes, George. I am here." He never asked if I was there; he seemed to be a great deal stronger than me. Perhaps he had been through this darkness before and wanted to support me through it.

I received tremendous comfort and assurance from Mike's voice. It was so close. Not many words were spoken, but the words he spoke were enough. Mike was there with me in the darkness. His presence gave me the strength to get through each day.

This memory is a recent one for me. It just arrived a few months ago. Having suffered years of abuse in my childhood, memories like these often surface one by one without warning. Why has it come back to me now?

Over the past few months, I have been reading the Gospel of John. John 6:16-21 caught my attention: "That evening Jesus' disciples went down to the shore to wait for him. But as darkness fell and Jesus still hadn't come back, they got into the boat and headed across the lake toward Capernaum. Soon a gale swept down upon them, and the sea grew very rough. They had rowed three or four miles-when suddenly they saw Jesus walking on the water toward the boat. They were terrified, but he called out to them, 'Don't be afraid. I am here!' Then they were eager to let him in the boat, and immediately they arrived at their destination!" (NLT).

Have you ever found yourself overcome with fear? Have you ever encountered such darkness and waves that you've cried out, "God, are you there?"

I'm in that place now. No, it's not the closet of my youth, but it sure feels like it as my wife, my sweet Lisa, faces the darkness of cancer. She hadn't been feeling well for quite some time. After many doctor visits, we found ourselves sitting in front of an oncologist. Not a place we ever thought we would be. I'm still a bit numb as I write this now.

Cancer is never a word you expect to hear. As soon as it was spoken, Lisa and I felt darkness closing in all around us. Crushing our hands together, we silently asked, "God, are you there? Did you hear these results? It's cancer, God. Cancer!"

At first, His answer seemed a bit foggy. As a believer, I know that He has promised He will never leave me. But at times, I still find myself fighting the darkness and asking, "Why God? Why does it seem that we have to go through one dark closet right after another? How much can we take?"

I now understand that remembering the darkness and loneliness I felt inside the closet at daycare is important for my present circumstance. It's a memory God has allowed to surface to bring me, and perhaps you, to a place of peace and comfort. To remind us that, in our dark times, we are not alone. He is there with us—never abandoning us and never forsaking us. Always giving us the strength to make it through. Hold on to that hope and truth and let it be your strength and comfort in your dark time.

It hasn't been easy, but Lisa and I are finding that place of peace in the darkness as we look to the light of our Savior. Yes, God is with us, and it's going to be okay, no matter the outcome. God is stronger than cancer. He is brighter than the darkest night. He is the healer and the redeemer of life. And He will see us through this dark season and the next.

"God, are You there?"

"Yes, I'm here, George. Don't be afraid."

Time, Love and Beautiful Hugs

This story was not planned; this is a continuation of the previous story, *Emotions*. I'm not sure if I have ever had a story to follow another story, but here it is.

After the exploration of emotions in the last story, I was not sure if I was ready for another adventure so quickly. My youngest daughter had decided that she and my three grandchildren were coming to the lake house for the weekend.

I arrived on Friday as usual, unpacked, and soon learned that my daughter was just minutes behind me. I was already exhausted from the week's work and was unsure of how engaged I would be. I had not made that commitment yet. Much of my exhaustion had come from the previous weekend of emotional engagement with my oldest daughter's children.

What was I going to do? Some comfort came in knowing I had a therapy session scheduled for Monday. I was still very drained but willing to give it a go.

They arrived, and we decided to get takeout at a local sub shop. Lisa and I went to pick up the order with two of our grandchildren; my daughter stayed at the house to take care of the baby. When they arrived, we greeted each other as usual with a very light hug, an almost side hug of sorts. That has been the norm for the entirety of our relationship, never much emotion, engagement, or connection. It's really not them but the amount that I was willing and able to give; it was truly all I could give.

I felt my heart was changing. I wasn't sure what was happening, but things seemed different. Did last weekend have such a profound effect on my innermost being that changes were still continuing? I think so.

I was cautious and not sure that opening the door on these new emotions was such a great idea. The therapist had recommended *cracking the door* to see what pain or fear might be in that room of emotions. I wondered if it would turn into another emotional withdraw as it had for so many years.

We talked as we drove to pick up the food, and as usual, it was just surface talk and nothing really engaging; I was happy with that at the moment.

On Saturday, the boys arose and said, "What's the plan?" To my surprise, they were ready for a day at the lake, and I was refreshed and ready to engage. We ate breakfast, and the plan was to hit the lake wide open, no matter what. I was ready to put forth an unconditional effort to show the boys that I love them, not by what I could buy them, but what mattered the most, time. Lisa kept telling me, "All they want is time," and time is all I have.

So now, this is a week later and I'm back to finish the story. When I write a story, I usually sit down and write what has played out in my mind for weeks or for months on end. This story has brought up so many emotions that I had to take a break. I know this is an unusual writing style, but I always want the reader to be here in this moment with me.

The boys wanted to go out on the boat, so we left the baby with Lisa. My daughter put on their life vests, and we headed out into the deep water where we could dive; the water is shallow at the dock. There was so much excitement in the boat; I was excited as well. I asked my daughter if she wanted to get a ski ride in because the water was smooth, and her answer was a quick, "Yes!" The boys enjoyed watching their mom rip it up, just like back in the day. Growing up, we spent most of our spare time on the water, and this is the very lake that I taught both my daughters how to slalom ski.

I was getting emotional watching her ski and so many memories were coming back. After she got back in the boat, we joked about the falls, the injuries, and the soreness that would come in the morning. Such a wonderful moment to go back in time.

The boys were getting restless and were ready to enjoy the water. The oldest is now twelve, his brother is eight-years-old, and the baby is a few months old.

I jumped in and they asked, "Can you touch? Can you touch?" I told them it was too deep; it was only about seven-feet deep. The youngest put his mask on, got on the boat platform, and looked down into the depths and said, "It's ok."

They jumped off the platform, climbing in and out of the boat. In years past, I would have sat in the boat or on the side of the boat, just watching and observing, being careful with my involvement. Today, I was in the water with them, climbing in and out as much as they were, and jumping and diving. My oldest grandson asked, "Can you watch me dive and tell me how to do that?"

My heart sank. *Time*, I thought, that's all, just time. That's where we were, on lake time. I gave a demonstration and then he tried his dive. "Perfect." I said. "Let's do it again." We dove again and again. He was already an excellent diver; I was helping him with some pointers. My daughter asked me who taught me how to dive. With sadness, I said, "I don't know."

Sitting here writing this today, I'm looking out over this beautiful place with tears in my eyes, wishing they were here right now; it's so breathtaking.

The youngest was doing some interesting and funny dives; he was making up dives he called *the fish, the alligator*, and some hilarious slides off the platform. He made me laugh. I was *cracking the door* and looking in these rooms of emotions and found that it was okay. It was okay to let myself experience these times, happy or sad; they were good.

We had to head back in as the sun was setting, and we were all hungry. They kept saying, "Just one more jump, just one more dive." We were having fun, and that's all that mattered. I wondered what the night would hold, how I would sleep, and if there would be a rush of emotions that I wasn't ready for in the dark of the night. Deep in my soul lies that child who has no memory, no emotions, and no love; these developmental years are missing. These children are teaching me these foundational truths, and they all start with time and that equals love. Time is love!

It's never too late to start. I'm here to say that, and maybe that's what this story is about. My oldest grandchild is twelve now, and it's not too late; I will explain why shortly.

Most of my family has been understanding with me over the years. My therapist has helped me gain new perspectives on my complex emotions and lack of development during my foundational years.

There are some in the family who don't understand and that's okay. They never had the struggles I've had. With that being said, every person alive has a struggle; we as individuals filter them out so no one else sees them. I know they are there; they are seen, and they will probably go to the grave with most.

Later that evening, my wife and daughter were doing a puzzle; they love those things. Me, not so much. I have a hard enough time putting my pieces together!

I was walking through the kitchen and just threw out a statement like, "Making progress; I'm making progress." My youngest daughter doesn't miss much, and as always, didn't miss that either.

"What are you talking about, Daddy?"

"Well, I'm cracking doors and looking in, engaging and loving, and giving time unconditional." I cried as I realized my heart was full, full of love of the time we all gave the boys that day. It's not about what you have, but about what you have to give. All they want is time. It was no longer about me but me giving time and giving love.

The next morning, we all got up and hit the water again, same as the day before but elevated to a new level. The oldest wanted to ski, so he got going. As my daughter was watching him, I could see her giving him instructions just like I did her back in the day. I cried, thinking that all I needed to give them was love and time. The youngest was cheering his brother on; he was so excited. When the boat stopped, he wanted to jump in again and again. I was all in at this point. We all dove and enjoyed the water, but it was time to go. One more dive, one more pencil dive, one more jump—this went on for a long time.

We climbed back onto the boat dock. Then the boys jumped out of the boat, only to jump off the dock again and again with their goggles on, searching for treasures. My wife and daughter told me they were heading to town to do some shopping, and the youngest said he was going with them. The oldest asked me if we could take the canoe out for a ride. I agreed, but in my mind, I was wondering what we were going to talk about. What was this going to look like? We have never spent much time alone. We got in the canoe, and I told him we could fish around the docks. We took one fishing pole and one worm; you can see I had a great deal of confidence in our catching ability. We pushed off the dock, and we both paddled to the next dock; he cast over in the distance, under the dock, over the dock, and we still weren't catching any fish.

I told him we would go out into the deep water and see if there were any fish out there. A beautiful light wind was blowing. He cast behind the boat, and we let the wind push us. Then the fish started to bite; we caught a couple and were excited. At one point, I lost my balance, and I fell out of the canoe. We laughed so hard. We walked back to the dock and got back in, soaking wet. I was a proud grandfather. What a great memory we created. We headed back out and took more worms with us, but the fish were just too small to catch. My daughter and wife returned, and my grandson screamed out that we had caught some fish. We went back to the dock and told the story of the mishap, and we all laughed. Cracking that door wasn't easy, but it's all about time and doing things they enjoy doing. Time is love, and love needs time. No matter the foundation issues early in my life, it's never too late and my experiences with my grandchildren are proof of that.

As they were getting ready to go back home, the oldest came up to me and gave me the best hug I've ever had; the youngest did the same. They were the most embracing hugs I've ever had. Not just one hug, but many full on beautiful, loving hugs, meant to tell me thank you for the time and thank you for the love I shared; I know it was hard, but it's okay.

I came back in the house and cried as they pulled away. The moments with my grandchildren made me feel loved and blessed. As I watched the sun go down that evening, I relived every moment in reverse, wishing they were still there. The house has been quiet this weekend, but I know in the future it will be full of time, love, and beautiful hugs.

Elaine's Pain, Part One

The voice on the phone said, "Did you hear about Elaine?" I replied, "No, what happened?" She explained that Elaine had died and that she had committed suicide. My heart sank deep, and sadness prevailed over my countenance. My heart ached with pain, and to this day, I am still sad about the life of Elaine.

Elaine was a sweet girl. She was beautiful with long blonde hair and a perfect build. Yet as pretty as she was, she had some deep-rooted pain that would often come out of her. Her pain usually came out in the form of rage after a few drinks. Looking back now, I recognize the pain she was carrying around. We often talked, but she never revealed the root of her pain to me.

For Elaine, it began in high school, as it often does with teenagers. She was part of the *smoking area* crowd and ranked high in this group. Elaine was the one in the group that would call out anyone and say a few choice words to explain herself. But apart from that, she was as sweet and gentle as any one woman could ever be. Her smile was beautiful, and she attracted many of the guys in the group. One of them was my friend, David.

David and I lived at the boy's home together; we were good friends and talked frequently about the issues of life. One hot summer's night, David came to me and said he needed to talk to me. His voice was shaky, and I could tell something was eating him up. So, we went outside the cottage and sat against the house. The moon was riding high that night, and I still remember the heat of the bricks on my back; this was the side of the house the sun hit most of the day. We both sat down with our backs on the warm bricks. He asked me about marriage and babies—things that neither of us were well-versed in. It didn't take long before David told me what all the questions were for.

"Elaine is pregnant." His voice was shaky and nervous. "What do I do?" he asked. The answers were not clear to either of us. We talked for several more hours, and he made a decision. David had to marry her; that was the only option, not because she was pregnant, but because he loved her. That was my only question to him. "Do you love her enough to marry her?" This I knew nothing about. Love to me was a distance word; my mom was the only one who had ever told me she loved me. Understanding the meaning of love was much too deep for me at the time.

Before you go all judgmental on me, both David and I were in our late teens and had no idea of what life was. But like most teens, we thought we knew it all. I was proud that David trusted me enough to hold his story, a story that would rock the high school and all the families involved. I was careful to guard it and not tell anyone. Even to this day, only a few of my friends know this story. I am not even sure if my best friend, Amy, knows. We never talk about Elaine.

David and Elaine married, and they had a son. This shook up the entire community in this small town. I was excited for David because he seemed to be happy. But inside, I think he was torn.

As you would expect, the marriage didn't last long. Elaine ended up back at the lake, and David joined the Army, searching for a better life. He later remarried and then divorced again.

David's pain was as deep as Elaine's. The root of his pain has never been addressed. He had only been treated for his symptoms, as we all had been back then. I was able to meet with David last year and talk about this deep-rooted pain that only Jesus can take away. We will hold David's story for another chapter.

Elaine and I remained friends through this, and she would eventually move to our town and move in with us. We fell in love and planned on getting married, but the story would soon take a tragic turn.

Before I go on to Chapter Two of *Elaine's Pain*, I feel led to ask a question to all who read this. What part of Elaine's pain are you carrying? I know you know a girl like Elaine—everyone does! Her pain is deep. Her laughter is sad. Her strength is weak. Her words are full, yet empty, and she is lost! Did you hear me? She is lost! Do you know her? Do you know where she is? Please find her and tell her Jesus loves her and wants to take her pain. Jesus is the only answer to our hurting and dying world.

Elaine's Pain, Part Two

Elaine and I continued in our relationship for several more months. Looking back now, I can see that our arguments were never about us but about what was eating at her inside. I knew nothing about her pain, only that I carried pain in my own life.

So many years have passed, and I miss Elaine from time to time. If you are carrying some deep-rooted pain, and if you have experienced a horrific, life-changing event, please get help. These events can lead to death and destruction. They are the events that have such a hold on you that it's hard to function in the world. They are the quiet secrets inside of us we never reveal to anyone. They will kill you if you let them.

Proverbs 16:6 (MSG) says, "Guilt is banished through love and truth." Condemnation is not from God; what happened in the past doesn't have to steer your life to a tragic end. As I told a great friend this past weekend, speaking truth sets free a condemning spirit; this is a spirit that will ultimately wreck your life. We must choose to speak in love and truth; every word that comes out of our mouths should be that of truth and love. If I knew then what I know now, things may have been different. But I know God made everything for a place and purpose. Every event, every word, every song, every smile, every hug, and every death has a purpose.

My only regret is I can't tell Elaine I'm sorry. I can't tell Elaine that I can help her. I can't tell her Jesus loves her, and God wants to restore her. I can't tell her God has a plan for her life. I can't give a hug. I can't give a smile. I can't give a kiss. I can't even give a word of encouragement. Elaine is dead.

Do you know an Elaine? Don't be so busy in your life that you can't call her. Don't be so busy you can't go to lunch with her. Don't be so busy you never hear her cry for help. I never heard her!

I am forever grateful to have known Elaine. One of the greatest tragedies is the fact that she lived down by the lake for so many years and her cries were never heard. Elaine's pain died with her. I love you, Elaine.

The Rope Swing

This is one I wrote in September 2006. Little did I know the real effect it would have on my life.

As I sat on the front porch today, looking at the two fifty-foot magnolias in front of our house, I could not help but think back a few years. I remember when I built Sara and Laura their very own rope swing; it still hangs there today, just swaying in the wind. Not much good for anything except memories now. The two-by-four ladder is the same way. It's still there, but is not being used anymore. These are the memories that take me back; they take me back to a starting point. I can still see them swinging there sometimes and still hear their voices calling from the tree. "Daddy, Daddy, look at me," they would yell. "Come climb the tree with me." I would always climb up and swing higher than they were allowed to swing.

I am telling you all this because during moments like these, we need to be reminded that the beginning of something holds the best memories. Sometimes, God wants us to go back to the start, not just for a moment but to reflect on that time of our lives, forget the details, and take a deep look at what He has done in our lives. It's a time to think about the people we have met, the lives that have been changed, and how God has molded us over the past years. Some things will shape us forever; for me, it is St. Louis. I am a different person because of what happened there. It is my forever *empty swing.* What could have happened didn't, and what should have happened did. I have to leave it at that. It's a memory now, but one that comes to me very often.

Our lives get so busy, we end up focusing on all the little details and lose sight of the goal. If we are not careful and keep a good balance, we end up sitting on the porch, looking at an empty swing and thinking, *I would give anything to swing one more time; I would give anything to climb one more time.*

God has shown me in the past weeks that His call on my life and the lives of all those here is so real and should not be tampered with. We have to do this! Lives are in the balance; souls are in the balance. So, as we go out this weekend doing the will of the Father, going from place to place, seeking the lost, healing the hurting, please remember those magnificent, majestic magnolias. They are just the keepers of the old rope swings, the old nailed-up ladder, and the wonderful memories of a season that was so full of joy. Remember the time you came here, when we all first met. We are all still the same people. We have just added a closet full of memories. How blessed are we?

So, when the swing gets empty, go to the Word and look up something that takes you back to the start. Let's take our time, seeking that one hurting soul who needs a life-changing touch. It may be that their swing is empty, and they need to remember back. It may be one of us.

Credible

Credible I am not.
I mean, what is credibility?
Does it make me great?
Does it make me better than the poor?
Credible I am not.
Poor I am.
No better than a stray dog.
No better than a cat with no home.
It doesn't make me cry.
It doesn't even make me sad.
I mean, I have it all.

Credible I am not.
Some say, "But you're a child of the King."
And I agree.
I would say, "Does that make me better than thee?"
Credible because we talk to the best.
We walk with the best.
We wear the best.

We live with the best.
Then who perceives?
The credible?
I say, "That's incredible!"
An incredible lie.
A lie that so many live.

So, let's break this down.
It's not credibility to the concerned.
It's the story of the incredible.
"What story?" you may ask.
The only credible One.

Jesus!
Born from a virgin.
Is that credible?
No, that's incredible.
Born with no home,
Born to die,
Born to sacrifice for you and I.
That's no lie.

"What the hell?" you may ask.
And I say, "That's the point."

Hell is real.
Credible it is.
Your credibility matters there.
But not here.

Now you see.
Credible I am not.
His story is!
My story is what it is.
Jacked up!
Misdirected and misunderstood,
Poor but rich,
Full of lies of existences.
Living the dream but living the lie,
The lie of credibility.

That's why I exist.
Credible not because of me.
It's because of He.
That's why I exist.
Because I'm on His list.
Credible I am not.
But home I will be.
Credible with Him,
In the end.
That's all that matters to me.

Will you be?

Please Leave a Review

Thank you for joining my journey! Now, a request: If you enjoyed the read, please be kind and leave a review on the site from which you purchased the book. Reviews greatly help both authors and readers, so I look forward to hearing how my book has influenced you.

You are welcome to visit my website and follow me on Facebook for more:

https://hopeinthestruggle.com/and

https://www.facebook.com/georgeandlisa.beasley

www.ingramcontent.com/pod-product-compliance
Lightning Source LLC
LaVergne TN
LVHW052302200926
848481LV00002B/440
* 9 7 9 8 9 9 6 7 4 3 7 0 4 *